Bindarra Creek
Makeover

A Bindarra Creek Romance

S. E. GILCHRIST

DEDICATION

For my wonderful children, Kerstie, Kyle and Blake – in good times and bad, you are always my soul.

For my mother for her courage and strength.

For my wonderful CP's & friends – Erin Moira O'Hara, Juanita Kees, Kerrie Paterson, Sandie James and Stacey Nash.

Having you all in my life is worth more than gold.

✱

Also by S. E. Gilchrist

Darkon Warriors series: *Legend Beyond the
Stars
The Portal
Awakening the Warriors
Star Pirate's Justice
When Stars Collide
Bargain with the Enemy
Touring the Stars
The Slave Trap*

Apocalyptic: *Paying the Forfeit
Storm of Fire*

Warders of Earth series: *Don't Look Back*

Mars Academy Series: *Stranded
Cosmic Fire*

Bound Series: *Bound by Love
Bound by Lies*

Contemporary: *Dance in the Outback
Cowboy under the Mistletoe*

Coming Soon: *The Cowboy's Gift
Desire for Love
Marnie's War*

ACKNOWLEDGMENTS

I would never have realised my dreams of being a writer without the motivation and support of my family, friends and the wonderful writing community, Romance Writers of Australia. Thankyou to my face-to-face writing group, Hunter Romance Writers – a wonderful bunch of ladies.

A special thankyou to my fellow members of the Bindarra Creek Romance series – it's been a fun, challenging and exciting ride and an absolute pleasure to share this particular journey with all of you.

✱

A Bindarra Creek Romance

Drama, intrigue, suspense, adventure and honest country goodness – welcome to Bindarra Creek where life and love in a small country town has never been more challenging.

*

BINDARRA CREEK MAKEOVER

CHAPTER ONE

"What we have here folks, is a genuine, once-in-a-life-time opportunity for Bindarra Creek." Tessa patted the impressive stack of papers piled square-edged on the podium in front of her.

Lips stretched wide in a pseudo confident smile, she gazed over the crowded Country Women's Association hall, taking careful note of the body language as she made eye contact with each towns-person.

Dammit! Judging by their folded arms and stiff upper torsos there were still a few skeptics in the crowd. And worse, a deep frown on the face of the guy sitting in the back row of cheap, plastic chairs. There was a twist to his lips that told her he wasn't buying what she was selling. All she could do was hope his late arrival meant he had little interest in her presentation and wouldn't put a spanner in the works.

He'd been one of the last to walk through the door and even though he wore no uniform, she'd known instantly he was a cop. The aura of authority that clung to him and the way he'd automatically scanned the crowd with a slow, considering stare had given him away. She'd been on the receiving end of similar looks in her teenager days when she'd lived rough and worked cleaning restaurant kitchens in return for food to survive after she ran away from home. Discovering she was pregnant followed soon after by the death of her boyfriend, Ian, in a street-car race had been her wake-up call. With the help of a kids' refuge in the Blue Mountains, she'd turned her life around.

But here she was again, full circle and desperate. No matter how sick she felt inside from her actions she'd see her plan through to the end. She'd almost lost her little girl twice – she couldn't risk a third time.

Her fingers curled over the wad of paper she'd made to project the impression of legitimacy and she shivered. Outside, the temperature had dropped to two degrees Celsius. The five radiators attached to the walls did little to warm the frigid air that crept inside from the open door and unadorned, ill-fitted windows that rattled with every gust of wind. With a vintage of 1920, she doubted any of the modern conveniences like insulation had been added to the hall. In fact, its rusting tin roof, and sagging, peeling weatherboards proclaimed little if no renovations had been carried out since it was first built. Seriously, she couldn't work out whether it was colder inside or out.

The cheap, summer-weight linen suit she'd purchased especially for tonight, was totally inadequate to ward off the chill that frosted the air but it was all she could afford these days. The cost of her daughter, Kaylee's medication was prohibitive and took every spare dollar out of her tight weekly budget. The specialist had reiterated how vital it was she continued the course he'd prescribed over the twelve months following her heart surgery. But a clerk's salary was small when you factored in the prohibitive cost of living in Sydney.

It was a no-brainer. Her daughter's health came first.

And now thanks to her stupid decision to go on a blind date with a guy she'd met on social media, she'd dragged her past into her present. If her daughter was to have a future, then they both needed to disappear and fast. But to do that successfully, she needed money.

For three terrible and terrifying weeks when she'd jumped at every shadow and every phone call, she'd thought and thought. Then, the Federal Government announced its latest initiative - rejuvenate country towns that could prove their needs for funds and ability to administer the grant. If she could somehow use her skills in evaluating the state government's funding for town councils, perhaps she could siphon some of that grant money her way. Two months later, here she was – ready to convince a town she was the best person to handle their grant application. She'd include a bit of chat about how with her connections she could fast track their application and ensure the council made her their representative. It should be easy enough to convince them the money needed to be funneled into a trust fund and make herself the main signatory. She'd leave the first installment alone and take the rest. Game over – except it wasn't a game.

It was a matter of protecting her child.

Kaylee would be safe.

And that bastard would never find them.

Useless to seek help from the police. She'd tried that avenue once before when she'd been thirteen. No one had believed the kid of a prostitute junkie, especially as the man she was accusing was a successful businessman with a lot of friends in high places. Besides, she'd often seen cops 'visiting' her mother.

No they couldn't be trusted. She was on her own.

Tessa regulated her breathing pattern and clenched her jaw to stop her teeth from chattering. The lure of a brief, hot shower after the meeting spurred her on. She rested her hands on top of the papers, keeping her body relaxed, giving her all in the riskiest gamble of her life.

Smile switched off, she pasted on her well-practiced serious and concerned expression saying earnestly, "I fully understand your reluctance to commit to this scheme, but when you weigh up the pros against the cons, you will see there is nothing to lose."

Two of the townspeople unfolded their arms and whispered to their neighbours. A good three quarters of the crowd now sported smiles and nodded their heads, some grinning inanely as if visions of dollar signs danced inside their heads.

Adrenaline fizzed through her veins like newly opened champagne. *I'm on the home run.* She'd been spruiking for a good hour and now it was time to reel in her catch.

Pausing, she tapped the papers in front of her. "The recent federal government's initiative to fund development in small rural towns like Bindarra Creek will not only encourage investment but provide a future for your children. No longer will they be forced to move to the Big Smoke in search of work. No, they will remain here with their families, marry and raise their children -your grandchildren - in what will become a thriving community."

She leaned forward. "I can make your dreams a reality. Together, we can bring this town back to life."

The hall erupted in a storm of clapping and wild cheering.

And that folks, is a sale.

Unable to stop herself, her eyes sought the copper at the far end of the room. No smile on his face. In fact, his cool stare snatched a little of the shine off the moment. She had a sinking feeling he intended to seek her out, probably ask a whole pile of cop-type questions she had no intention of answering honestly. And at the moment, her disgust for the situation she'd locked herself into was like bricks weighing her down. The last thing she needed right now, was that discerning gaze examining her face, peeling aside her secrets.

Heart thumping, she dragged her eyes from his and smiled at the councilmen seated on the stage.

Her added, "Thank you for taking the time to listen" was drowned out by the excited crowd but Tessa didn't care. She was drained, her underarms sticky with sweat. She wanted nothing more than to escape to her motel room and haul warmer clothes over her cold body. She'd take out her latest photo of Kaylee and remind herself of all she had to lose.

She looked over again and saw the cop shouldering his way toward her. Her heart rate sped up again. She needed to leave now, before the cop had a chance to collar her.

The district Mayor, a middle-aged guy named Donaldson, rose from his chair beside the podium and with both arms outstretched as if to embrace her, bounded forward. He was surprisingly nimble considering the girth of his protruding belly. Tessa neatly evaded the hug and shook his hand.

"First thing tomorrow...say nine-thirty," he boomed. "We'll meet to discuss your proposal in detail. You're staying at the Akuna Motel, aren't you?"

Tessa nodded.

"Excellent, excellent." He rubbed his hands together. "We'll meet in their dining room with the others. I especially want the members of this district's oldest families to be present. You're good for tomorrow aren't you, Charlie?"

Grinning, the mayor smacked a fellow councilman, a wizened old codger who looked as if he'd already passed his first century, on the shoulder.

Glad to be spared the enthusiastic back pounding, Tessa turned aside to gather up her papers and folders then packed them neatly into her briefcase. The locks snicked shut with a satisfying click.

The mobile she'd left lying on the podium vibrated.

Her pulse spiked. Quickly she snatched it up and answered. "Yes?" But the voice on the other end wasn't who she feared. A little of the constriction in her chest dissolved as she listened. Smiling, she nodded then said huskily, "I miss you too sweetheart. I'll be home soon."

She ended the call and pocketed her phone.

"That was a very smooth speech you gave, Miss Gibson," drawled a male voice as rich and intoxicating as home-brewed whiskey. "Full of an awful lot of words which really when it comes down to it, were as empty as old Wilson's bore. It sounded like a typical politician's speech to me. Brimming with promises. Light on detail."

Tessa knew without turning, the voice belonged to the guy her instinct told her was a cop. *Relax, remember what's at stake.*

Her gut churned at being so close to the law but to ignore him would send up a signal she had no wish to flag. She didn't want to give him any reason to run a check on her background. But she'd keep the contact brief and wiggle out from under his crystal-sharp gaze as quickly as possible. So, instead she hoisted her briefcase into her right hand and sidestepped to face him. One eyebrow raised and smoothing down the beige suit jacket with her other hand, she gave a polite smile. "I'm sorry and you are?"

"Constable Dylan Myers but most people call me Dodge." He jerked a thumb behind him and Tessa saw a heavily pregnant, blonde woman in a police uniform with sergeant stripes standing with a group of elderly townspeople. "Lou and I run the local cop shop here in Bindarra Creek."

Tessa remembered the policewoman had been with the first lot of people to arrive which would explain why she was still in uniform. Probably had come straight from work.

"You surprise me. I thought a town with such a small population would be overseen by the police station in Moree or Armidale."

"You've done your homework." His long, slow perusal of her body sent fresh prickles of warning skittering down her spine like frenzied scorpions.

"Not really." Tessa managed an airy wave. "Evaluating census forms was my job for a long time. It's amazing what information your brain stores without realising it."

Crap. I just broke another golden rule of Ian's. Never give away personal information. No matter how trivial. To backtrack would only serve to highlight her error. Better to move on – quick smart.

The constable planted his hands on his slim hips and studied the excited townspeople.

Any minute, he'd fix those serious, hazel eyes of his back onto her. *Move feet!* To her dismay, her feet remained glued to the floor and her gaze riveted to his profile and the soft, golden-brown hairs of the five o'clock shadow lining his chiseled jaw. The collar of his navy-blue parka was turned up, the end points nudging his firm chin. He had straight, light brown hair cut short and slightly tousled. Her fingers twitched as she fought the urge to smooth the strands into order. His shoulders were totally sigh-worthy and appeared wide enough to carry any amount of weight.

The guy was gorgeous and younger than she'd first thought. Up this close, she could see how unlined his smooth, light-olive skin was apart from laughter crinkles at the corners of his eyes. She doubted he had yet to see his thirtieth birthday.

And probably married already with half a dozen kids.

And she had a job to finish.

This is not like me, anyway, drooling over some strange guy. Besides men didn't play a role in her life, never mind how sexy they were. Look what had happened the last time, she'd taken a step in that direction!

She'd never forget that horrifying moment when she'd looked up from where she sat in the restaurant and stared into the face of her nightmare. Older, still fit and good-looking in a haggard, world-weary sort of way, his dark hair shot with silver and those icy, lifeless grey eyes that seemed to snare her soul – she'd recognize him anywhere.

For one heart-stopping moment, she'd prayed desperately he had no idea who she was but then he said her name. About to flee he'd sensed her intention and had grabbed hold of her wrist, twisting her flesh painfully but she didn't wince. Didn't cry out. Knowing from past experience how he'd loved to hear her plead. His fingers had dug deeper all the while smiling pleasantly, oozing that charm of his that so skillfully disguised the mire of darkness that swirled beneath. Then he'd spoken.

God but she still could hear his voice inside her head, like an echo of all the vile things he'd said all those years ago.

"Relax, Tessa. You're too old for me now. I've found someone I like much, much more."

Continuing to smile, he'd flicked in front of her face a photo Tessa had posted on Facebook last Christmas.

Clad in a hospital gown, a huge smile on her face was Kaylee - her beautiful little girl.

Blinking furiously, she dragged her thoughts away from the past and her gaze away from the cop. She clawed in a shaky breath. Taking four steps past him, she relaxed as she spied the exit a few metres away. The floorboards creaked, making her wonder whether they'd give way at any moment. Seriously, this place was a dump.

A woman in her late sixties and with grey hair flowing freely to her waist, darted in front of her.

Without a by-your-leave, she grabbed Tessa's left hand and held it close to her aquiline nose.

Tessa smiled politely while every nerve in her body jittered with the need to flee. "Excuse me, may I help you?" She tugged her hand.

The other woman's fingers dug in harder as she peered into Tessa's palm. "A child with blood staining her chest. Black shadows cloud your past and obscure your future. Where are the rainbows?"

Tessa's knees shook. *What was this crap?*

The woman dropped Tessa's hand as if scalded and her green-brown eyes drilled into Tessa's face. "Death rides close by your side," she said, slowly.

She can't know. How could she? Hands shaking, Tessa brushed past, never minding how rude she might appear. She rushed to the door and shoved through, desperate to escape.

The icy night air hit her lungs, stinging with every breath she took. The old woman had described her situation perfectly. It was uncanny and scared her. Her black patent leather shoes clattered in the quiet, as Tessa hurried down the brick steps and onto the path. Footsteps sounded behind her. Heart pounding, she half-turned and found the copper coming up fast.

"Crazy old bat. She should be locked up." The words born from the fear still clutching at her heart, tore from her mouth before she could stop them.

"That was my gran," he said in an even tone that effectively masked any emotion he might be feeling.

Heat bloomed over her face doing nothing to fight the chill eating into her bones. Unable to think of anything to say that wouldn't make matters worse, Tessa clamped her lips shut.

The silence stretched as they stood. She could feel his gaze drilling into the top of her head as she looked blindly down at the cracked pavement. Why had he followed her?

"I'd like to know a bit more about the service you're offering."

I should have known. Cops are hard to fool. She raised her head and met his shadowed gaze. "The mayor has all the information and I intend to answer any concerns at tomorrow's meeting. Perhaps you could join us?" *Please, please say 'no'.*

"I might drop in, if I get the chance."

Tessa cast a disparaging glance around the dark streets. "Hardly a hot-bed of crime, is it?"

"There's always something going on, even in a town as small as Bindarra Creek," he said mildly. "Why us? Why Bindarra Creek?"

Deciding a little honesty would go a long way, Tessa admitted, "I saw an advertisement in *The Land* and when I was commissioned to do up grant proposals for some reason the name of your town popped into my head." No need to mention how she'd researched the town thoroughly ensuring it ticked all her boxes. The prime box being a small town desperate enough not to check too closely into her credentials.

The breeze picked up and Tessa shivered.

"Need a lift to the motel?" he said.

"No, thank you. I have a rental car." She indicated the Toyota sedan parked in the street.

"No worries. Catch you tomorrow then." He turned and re-mounted the steps to disappear inside the hall. Back where there was light and a solid community waiting for him.

Shivering and alone, she stared down the dark, empty road feeling the night press in on her, from every side.

The shrill yap of a fox on the outskirts of town, cut through the quiet making her jump. Close to tears, she stumbled to the car and slid behind the steering wheel. *Focus on the big picture. You can do this.*

Head held high, she started the engine and drove along the street past the Royal hotel with its one lit window. She assumed the publican and his usual patrons were still at the hall talking about her proposition. A thought that made her smile as she swung the wheel, taking the first turn to the left onto Main Road.

Mist speckled the windscreen like scattered tears and she flicked on the wipers. She turned right at the only roundabout where the cenotaph with its roll-call of the dead, stood in the centre. She swept past the imposing bank on the corner built from convict bricks and drove along Mount Ingalls Road.

The street was deserted save for a possum that scampered across the road in front of her no doubt making for the relative safety of the park on her right. The possum's eyes shone eerily in the beams of the headlights. It was lost behind the car as she drove on, passing a run-down two storied building on her left, a couple of houses that looked abandoned next to a dirt road and then paddocks. The motel was on the same side of the road as the RSL club and its carpark bordered a lonely section of town that petered out to vacant lots and fields. It was clean if outdated with its orange and green decor. The owners definitely had their feet still rooted in the seventies. Hell, the whole town appeared to be rooted in the past.

She eased off the accelerator, turned the car into the Akuna Motel driveway and parked in the lot. When the engine faded into silence, she heard the croaking of frogs from the river even through the car's closed windows. A dog burst into a volley of barks, sparking a row from others close by.

Cattle bellowed in a nearby field.

Welcome to the country.

She sighed as she walked down the path, heading for her room situated at the end of the building and hopefully a good night's sleep. The crisp air filled her lungs with the tangy scent of eucalypt and pine mixed with cow manure. Her spirits lightened as if buoyed by the heady smells of country life, so far away and so different to the smog, bustle and blare of western Sydney.

She could do this, all she had to do was remain focused.

Her mobile buzzed, signaling a message.

As soon as she reached her door a sensor light came on and she slid her phone into her hand. Caller ID unknown. She read the text.

I know where you live.

The phone fell through her nerveless fingers.

Her heartbeat drummed in her ears. Bile scorched her throat. Clutching her heaving stomach, Tessa bent over and battled to control her terror.

Kaylee.

CHAPTER TWO

"She's trouble." Inside the still crowded CWA hall, Edwina Lette stuck a rolled smoke between her lips and lit up. Puffing furiously for a few seconds, she sucked in one long, deep breath and held it.

"Gran, you do remember I'm a cop? I could charge you with possession and use of an illegal substance." Dodge rocked back on his scuffed hiking boots. Holding back his grin, he considered the woman who'd played a more important role in his life after his mother died when he was twelve.

His gran noisily released a thin stream of smoke. "Medicinal. Helps my arthritis." She stole a quick glance at his face before turning away to inspect the crowd. "Don't change the subject. You know she's trouble."

"Yeah." The young woman had set his internal cop antenna quivering, along with various other parts he had no intention of admitting to his nosy grandmother. He'd never seen such long slim legs ending in a very enticingly tight butt nicely high-lighted by her clinging skirt and tight-fitted jacket. And those dark brown eyes of hers, like mocha-coffee. He could have stared into them for hours. Pity he'd spotted what he sure as hell thought were secrets lurking in those rich depths.

He cleared his throat. "The mayor reckons she's legit. He checked out her credentials before inviting her here."

Gran snorted. "Barry Donaldson has about as much street savvy as a rooster and everyone knows how dim they are. If she stays here, she'll bring trouble to the town."

"I can't see her staying for too long. She'll do her job and high-tail it back to the city as fast as she can."

"Maybe." Gran frowned. "Pity though. She's a pretty girl. Bindarra Creek could do with more young women, pretty or otherwise."

"Girls like her don't like the country."

"Pwush."

"Whatever you're plotting, forget about it," Dodge said, narrowing his eyes.

"You can't blame me for wanting to see a great grandkid or two before I die."

"You're as strong as a horse, so don't try that one on me."

"Have you asked that nurse, Miss Scott, out to dinner yet?"

"I've been busy. Besides, she doesn't give the impression she's looking for a bloke."

"What? Do you think women go around with a sign on their chest, saying 'here I am, take me'? Honestly, Dylan Myers, do I have to draw you a picture?" Gran sighed dramatically before inhaling another drag on her smoke.

Heat crawled up his throat. Trust his gran to bring up his love life or the lack of, any chance she could get. He did just fine the way he was, single with a close-knit family consisting of his grandmother, father and cousins and some good mates. He didn't need another woman telling him what to do in his life. Not at the moment anyway, not when he needed to sort out the mess his job had turned into. He had yet to make up his mind whether or not to resign and pursue a different career.

"Put that bloody thing out will you?" Dodge turned away to greet the woman waddling toward them. "Hey, Lou. How you feeling?"

"Good thanks. But you know you can stop asking me every five minutes." Louise Baker patted her rounded stomach and smiled at Edwina. "I like the sound of this grant. If it's approved, this could be a new beginning for Bindarra Creek."

Two elderly women flanked Lou on either side, matching bookends with their greying hair, pale, green eyes and limp clothes.

"Mrs Brown, Miss Collins," Dodge murmured.

"How exciting," Miss Collins said in her soft, gentle voice. She hugged her sparse frame clad in a fraying yellow jumper and patched woollen trousers and peered through her wispy fringe at them. "So lovely, if the children and grandchildren move back to town. It'll be just like old times, when we were young."

"Don't carry on like a fool, Beatrix. You've got no children," her older sister said.

"Oh, but I mean for the others." Miss Collins trembled where she stood, her timid gaze darting from her sister's stern face to Dodge then onto his grandmother.

Gran scowled. "I agree. Leave her alone, Pam."

"Not only is smoking harmful to the health, but what you smoke is illegal, Edwina. You should arrest her, Dylan."

Not for the first time, did he wish his grandmother's old friend would mind her own business. Biting down the words he longed to say, Dodge muttered, "It's medicinal."

"Poppycock," Mrs Brown bit out.

"I've got medical records to back it up."

Dodge wondered whether he should make a run for it before the conversation turned into another battle between the two strong-willed, old women who stood bristling at each other like fighting cocks. You'd never think by the way they carried on, they'd been friends since childhood.

"So you say." Pamela Brown sniffed. "That girl who was here; do you think she was the one asking all those questions in that email?"

"Oh be quiet, Pam." Gran glared at her friend.

"What? You know her?" Dodge eyed Mrs Brown.

"Never seen her before in my life. There's Esther, I must have a word with her about those new books that arrived in the library this week. Far too raunchy." Mrs Brown marched off to engage another elderly woman in a discussion Dodge knew from experience would be totally one-sided. Her sister murmured a vague goodbye and drifted after her.

Pamela Brown was a force to be reckoned with and one that most people had learned to avoid whenever possible. It didn't matter that she was seventy years old, when you saw her coming, you ducked for cover. There was nothing about this town, she didn't know.

Scenting a conspiracy, Dodge frowned. "What's going on, Gran?"

"You're wasted as a policeman. Too much imagination." Gran threw the remains of her smoke onto the floor and ground it out with the heel of her gumboot.

Lou laughed and nudged Dodge with her bony elbow.

"Oh Edwina, I wish you wouldn't do that." As if out of thin air, the rector's wife, Mrs Florence Miller, materialized in a pink floral dress with a worn, waterproof, leather stockman's coat thrown casually over her shoulders like a cape. She tutted over the crushed butt.

"Since I mop this place out every morning, I think I can do as I please."

"I *am* president of the CWA."

"Never mind that, Florrie, what's the rector have to say about this idea?"

Florence beamed. "Dear Jonas is beside himself. He's hoping a tad of the money could be diverted to the *Save the Church* fund."

"It's infested with rats," Gran said bluntly.

Florrie paled and clasped her hands together as if about to pray. "I know but the historical significance of the building can't be denied. You know how keen he is to restore the stained-glass windows." She paused, looking toward the door. "Such a nice speaking voice, but did you notice her eyes? So sad and wary, like a frightened deer."

Dodge glanced toward the door. Yeah, he hadn't missed that expression either. For all her composure, she was too contained, too careful with her body language and to a cop, that could mean only one thing – she was hiding something.

Gran didn't respond instead she raised her palms and gazed into them.

"Practicing your witchcraft are you Mrs Lette?" boomed Donaldson. Chuckling, he clapped a heavy hand to Dodge's back.

"It's Ms Lette and you know it."

Dodge rolled his eyes. *I should have left when I had the chance.*

Frowning, Donaldson sniffed the air like a hunting dog and Dodge cringed inwardly hoping the guy hadn't picked up the scent of Gran's smoke. Mercifully the mayor refrained from commenting, saying, "This is a good day for the people of Bindarra Creek." He puffed out his chest.

"We haven't got the money yet," pointed out Gran.

"No, no, no, that is true but you can't deny we've got a solid case in our favour."

Dodge laughed. He couldn't help it. "Oh come on!"

"Mark my words Constable, we'll have that money in Bindarra's coffers before the month is out. I had a little chat with that girl before she gave her speech. With her connections, it's in the bag."

"What connections?" His internal radar pinged again. To Dodge, it sounded like total bull crap.

Donaldson wagged a finger. "A policeman is always on the job, eh, constable? There's nothing to worry about. Everything is *kosher*."

Gran held out her hand. "I need her mobile number."

"I don't see why," Donaldson huffed.

"CWA business and you know we run this town."

"Fine." He fished a pen and his own business card from his pocket. After consulting his mobile, he scribbled on the card before handing it over. "Don't you go scaring the girl off, now. We need her."

He strutted off, greeting people left and right. "Mr Reid, glad you could make it into town. How you feeling these days?" His voice faded as he moved further into the press of people all anxious to discuss the grant and their eagerness to spend the government money.

"Now I *am* worried. If the mayor thinks this girl is above board then there's bound to be some shonky business going on." Dodge switched his gaze to the card held in Gran's hand. His fingers twitched. He so wanted to snatch it up and stuff it into his pocket. A notion that made him scowl.

"Do you think so, Dodge?" Mrs Miller's worried gaze followed the mayor.

"Yeah, I do." He looked at the rector's wife and gave a disbelieving snort. "No government ever works that fast. Even if the grant is approved, we'd be lucky to see any money this side of Christmas. No." He shook his head, face grim. "There's something more going on here and I intend to find out what it is."

"I know...we'll invite that girl to breakfast before she meets with the council members. You can ask her some 'cop' type questions. I'll phone Rhiannon Scott to pick her up and she can come along too." His grandmother rubbed her hands together. "We wouldn't want the poor girl getting lost now do we? This will give you the perfect opportunity to talk to Rhiannon."

"Gran!" groaned Dodge, feeling heat steal up his neck and over his face, again. Hooking a finger under his collar, he tugged it loose.

His gran smiled, looking smug as she placed the business card inside her handbag. "Nothing beats a good old-fashioned, home-cooked meal. This grant girl looked more bones than flesh. She could do with a decent feed. I hear money's tight for the McLeans. They serve up nothing more than corn flakes and toast to their guests."

"I'll come along too and bring Beatrix and Pam and some freshly potted marmalade," inserted Florence Miller, excitement shining in her eyes like stars.

"This, I can't wait to see. Count me in." Lou elbowed Dodge in the ribs again, her grin positively wicked.

Dodge sucked in a deep breath, his nostrils flaring. "Right then, why don't you invite the whole damn town?"

Gran chortled and patted her pockets as if searching for another smoke. "Now, now, don't get miffed. You leave it to me. I'll have a nice young girl in your bed before you know it."

Jaw working furiously, Dodge raised his eyes heavenward and prayed for patience.

CHAPTER THREE

Heart pounding, her breath sawing in and out of her throat, she plunged out of the up-scale bar and onto the pavement teeming with Friday night after-fivers determined to celebrate the end of their working week.

His social media profile said he was thirty-one years old, had a degree in commerce and worked as a real estate agent.

Lies. All lies.

A few shot curious glances her way but she ignored them. She pushed through the high-spirited crowd using her elbows, her shoulders, ramming her way metre by metre toward the taxi rank, its sign signaling hope, safety. Expecting any second to feel a heavy hand land on her shoulder. Haul her back.

Back to the nightmare she'd left behind all those years ago.

Never as long as she lived, could she forget him and what he'd done. That one terrible day was carved in her memory as indelible as her DNA.

Overhead, thunder rumbled. The lights from the bars and restaurants lining the street opposite were a glittering blur of colour through the rain hammering down on Darling Harbour. Sweat from more than the high humidity slicked her skin. Her teetering high-heels slipped when she stepped into a puddle and she staggered. Someone grabbed her elbow, stopping her from a nasty fall but she pulled away in terror.

"Hey, you okay?" he asked, peering into her face.

It's not him!

Mouth shaking, she forced down nausea and mumbled, "I'm fine. Thank you."

Head down, she darted on shaky legs around two heavily-tattooed young women, arms around each other leaning in for a kiss, and putting on a spurt of desperate speed reached her goal. A quick glance down the street revealed a taxi several cars away and heading in her direction. Holding her arm in the air, she waved frantically. The taxi flicked on its indicator and she knew the driver had spotted her.

From behind, a man shouted. Called her name. Raw fury in his voice.

Oh God. He was coming. She had to make certain he couldn't follow her.

The taxi was still three cars away.

She stepped out onto the road.

Heart pounding, Tessa fought free of the last clutches of sleep. The straggling rays of dawn filtered through the thin curtains, highlighting the drabness of the room to Tessa's gritty eyes. It was only a dream.

No, who was she kidding? It was the memory of when she'd come face-to-face with her past.

So much for getting a good night's sleep. Her mouth twisted. At least the shower last night had been scalding hot although her allotted six minutes had zipped past way too fast, but she appreciated water was a premium here where they hadn't had a good rainfall for over eight months.

She rolled onto her side, reaching for her phone to check for messages. *None.* The constriction in her chest relaxed and she flopped onto her back frowning up at the mould that flecked the ceiling.

It was possible the bastard had been messing with her mind. And how did she know the text had been from him anyway? She hadn't given him her number and it was unlisted. She didn't own a car, so she couldn't be traced through registration. But then, who else would send such a threatening text?

Maybe he found my address through my driver's licence? Or the electoral role? Kaylee – I need to check on her again, warn Maki to be extra careful. Grabbing her mobile again, she checked the time. Still too early to call. She'd sent a text last night asking if everything was okay but there was nothing like hearing the sound of your loved ones' voices.

Huddling under the thick doona, she forced her dread to the back of her mind. She needed to focus on her job and reflect on the townspeople's reaction the night before.

From what she'd seen on her drive through the town yesterday, the place could really do with an influx of funds. She squirmed, hating the uneasy prick of her conscience. It wasn't as if any of them were starving or desperate.

Never become emotionally involved with an intended mark. Ian's old mantra resounded inside her head. Instead of the familiar hot rush of bitterness twisting her heart, a dull sadness overladen with resignation settled on her. She clutched the covers, blinking rapidly against the burn of tears. *I've moved on. Forgiven him for leaving me. But he did give me the greatest gift of my life. My little girl. One I need to keep safe, no matter the cost to anyone else.*

On that thought, Tessa flung off the doona and scrambled to her feet, swinging her arms to increase her blood flow. She was ready, ready for whatever the day would bring and ready to fight anything and anyone to achieve her goal.

Her breath formed frosty puffs from the chilly room. Sighing, she looked sourly at the broken radiator before decided another shower was in order. Then she'd work her way through her usual morning yoga routine.

Forty minutes later she was dressed in skinny-leg blue jeans, a white woollen jumper and her long, dark-mahogany hair neatly brushed and braided into a side-plait. Her phone buzzed. Quickly she snatched it up and read the message from a Ms Lette. *Breakfast meeting at Fig Tree Lodge. Will arrange Scott to pick u up at 7.30am.*

Her eyebrows rose. *Interesting. A pre-meeting before the official meeting.* Her fingers tapped an uneven beat on the well-polished timber dresser as she stared at her reflection. Searching her memory, she came up blank. She was positive she hadn't been introduced to a 'Ms Lette' and wondered who she could be. *I hope she isn't that copper's grandmother.* Tessa shuddered, wryly admitting she'd do anything to avoid another encounter with the creepy woman. All that talk about blood and death was way too close to home.

Still an insight into the community could well give her added ammunition for her meeting with the mayor and his councilmen. *Know the enemy,* another of Ian's sayings. And this time, she smiled grimly as her confidence returned.

She texted her acceptance and hastily applied a light foundation, mascara and tangerine-coloured lipstick. After shoving her socked feet into her knee-high brown leather boots, she checked the contents of her large handbag for her small container of illegal Mace and decided she was ready for action. A glance at the phone told her she had ten minutes to spare.

Briefcase in hand, handbag slung over her shoulder, she snatched up the key and locked the motel room behind her. She'd decided to take a look around the area while she waited to be picked up by someone called Scott. And in the meantime, she had an important call to make.

Kaylee answered on the second ring as Tessa strolled through the carpark and then right onto the road.

"Mummy!" Her excited voice sounded over the kilometres separating them and Tessa experienced that painful twinge in her heart that represented a combination of love, protectiveness and mother's guilt. She hated being apart from her daughter like this, but she'd made her decision. What she was doing was for the best for her little girl.

Pausing to gaze out over a paddock studded with black and white cows, Tessa said, "Hello sweetheart. Are you dressed for school?"

"Yep. Maki made me *okayu* for breakfast."

"That's good. Did you do your homework last night?"

"Mum."

Tessa smiled at the groan in her daughter's tones. "I take that as a no. You know you've got a lot to catch up on." Due to follow up doctor's appointments, her daughter had missed a fair chunk of school this year.

"I guess," Kaylee grumbled.

"Tonight then, that's a good girl." Tessa deliberately kept her voice calm. "Remember, don't go talking to any strangers."

A white bird swooped down and landed on one of the cow's back. Amazingly, the animal didn't seem to mind, it kept munching away on spindly tufts of grass.

An exasperated huff sounded loud and clear over the phone.

"Alright then. Love you heaps. Can I talk to Maki now please?"

"Love you too, Mummy. Will you be home soon?"

"Soon, sweetheart."

"Okay. Here's Maki."

"'Lo?" said Makishi.

"How's it going?"

"All good," came his placid singsong voice.

"Keep a close eye on her, Makishi. And ring me if you notice anyone hanging around."

Silence.

Then, "Trouble?"

"Could be. I received a text message saying whoever it was knew where I lived. It may not even be from him but I can't think who else it could be. Just don't take any chances, please."

"I will do as you request, *Chan*."

Tessa smiled at the endearment. "Thank you." She ended the call, stuffing the phone into her handbag. God, where would she be without Maki? Probably dead in a ditch by now, if truth were told.

After Ian had died in that stupid race, she'd wanted so badly to find a different life for her unborn child. Then she'd heard on the streets about a refuge run by a Father Brian in Blackheath. She'd turned up to what was really a working farm, hardly daring to believe they would help her. But they had – she'd found a haven, been given a chance to train for work and met Maki working there as a gardener. Born to a Japanese mother and American father at the end of the WWII, he'd emigrated to Australia with his mother when he was twenty. Now, he worked at the refuge for room and board. The moment Tessa met him, they'd clicked and soon he became much more – he became family.

He was the only one she'd confided in about her past.

And the only one she'd entrust her daughter with - so as soon as she'd put her plans in motion, she'd called him.

Tessa lifted her face toward where the sun now peeped over the tree-studded slopes to the east. Pale rays spread across the fields making the frost-coated grass glisten with strands of gold. A flock of yellow-crested, white cockatoos burst shrieking from their perches in the trees and in a flurry of flapping wings raced across the sky. They called to each other like a school-yard of squabbling children. A mob of six kangaroos raised their heads to look on in mild curiosity. One of them turned to stare in Tessa's direction. Fascinated, she watched its ears flicker and swivel as if seeking sounds of danger. Apparently reassured, the roo scratched under its left armpit and showed large teeth in a massive yawn.

Giggling, Tessa dived into her handbag for her phone but by the time she had it in her hand and the camera activated, the roo had resumed its grazing. Still, she took the shot anyway and immediately forwarded it onto Kaylee.

A powder-blue Ford Focus pulled up beside her, engine humming quietly. Turning around, Tessa saw a dark-haired woman looking over the dashboard at her. The woman smiled and lifted a hand, indicating the passenger door.

With one last appreciative glance at the tranquil scene, Tessa strode to the car and upon opening the door slid onto the seat, placing her bags by her feet.

"Hi. Tessa Gibson I assume? I'm Rhiannon Scott, your guide on this lovely, frosty morning."

Tessa searched Rhiannon's face, feeling an instant liking for the young woman whose friendly, warm nature glowed in her brown eyes and wide smile. "Thanks for picking me up. I appreciate the lift."

Rhiannon laughed as she switched on the indicator and turned the car around. "You'll soon learn this town is run by the CWA. When those ladies say 'jump', we all fall in line."

"Sounds like they have a lot of say here," Tessa said thoughtfully and gazed out the window. In the park, a white-haired bloke muffled up to his neck with a brown scarf raked up fallen leaves while a chunky, blue heeler ran up and down barking at a pair of rosellas pecking in the grass.

"Pretty much but they have the town's best interests at heart."

"How long have you been here?"

"Not that long, a little over three months." Rhiannon slowed the car and checked both sides of the street, before driving straight through the intersection. "I'm a Sydney girl actually."

"And...?" Raising her eyebrows, Tessa tilted her head.

"It's good. The people are lovely, mostly. There usually is some old curmudgeon who tries to make a nurse's life difficult." She pointed to her uniform.

"I didn't know the town had a hospital."

"It doesn't. It's a polyclinic." Rhiannon frowned. "The clinic desperately needs more equipment. An upgrade would be wonderful. Old Charlie Walker fell from his ladder four weeks ago when he was clearing his eaves and he had to be airlifted to Armidale. He's such a nice old guy, happy to lend a helping hand to anyone that asks. Doctor Warner treated him on scene and since I was working in his surgery at the time, I went with him."

She shook her head. "I was worried he wouldn't make it, what with his dicky heart. If the town gets this grant, more injuries could be treated right here in Bindarra Creek without the risk of the delay it takes getting to Armidale. Urgent cases have to be choppered out or wait for the Royal Flying Doctor service which all adds up to wasted valuable time when someone's life is on the line. I'd love to see more beds available, an ex-ray department perhaps but more importantly, a fully equipped birth centre."

Enthusiasm laced her voice. She turned a serious face toward Tessa. "As you can imagine, there's not a lot to do here for the kids. Employment is practically non-existent. They're either getting into trouble or getting pregnant."

"Uh huh." Tessa shifted in her seat and pretended to be absorbed in picking flint from her jeans. *These people are nothing to you.*

"That's where I come in. I'm a midwife."

"What made you decide to come here? Do you have family living in town?"

"No particular reason. Well, here we are."

Tessa raised her eyebrows. Was it her imagination or did the other woman's friendly manner suddenly cool?

The car glided to a stop outside a genuine wrought-iron fence enclosing an enormous block of land. Rusting and with several panels missing, the fence sagged here and there as if weary from the toll of standing upright for far too many years. The wide double gates to the driveway were open and weeds grew thick and tall through the bars making Tessa wonder whether the gate had ever been closed.

An elderly Morris and a 1960-odd Landrover were parked out the front.

Exactly, how many people were invited to this breakfast meeting?

She tightened her grip on her briefcase and climbed from the car to follow Rhiannon who was already striding up the drive as if keen to escape any further questions.

Her footsteps crunched on the gravel drive that curved around surprisingly green grass that needed mowing. An enormous fig tree spread its massive branches over a good section of the front yard. Ferns and agapanthus had been planted around the base of the tree and in between the twisting root system. She could imagine a tyre swing swaying gently from its rope or picnicking under the tree's shade during summer. From somewhere amongst the heavy canopy of leaves, a currawong trilled into song competing with the chirping of other birds she couldn't name. On both fence lines, three River Red Gums grew tall and majestic and even from this distance she noticed the hollowed branches that proclaimed their age.

Her steps slowed as Tessa allowed her gaze to drift over the impressive two storied building. She'd always admired the historical homes in the older suburbs of Sydney and could well envisage how magnificent this house must have been in its heyday.

Something heavy settled in the region of her heart as she drank in the aura of solidness, strength and timelessness. The house was a rectangular structure built from old red brick, with wide verandahs surrounding it on all sides and wrought iron balustrades fencing in a similar verandah on the upper level. The timber windows were all double hung and looked freshly painted in cream. Several empty paint cans were jumbled off to the side of the wooden front door where Rhiannon waited. Two pet bowls filled to the brim with water were evidence that animal lovers lived here.

"Not bad, is it?" the midwife said.

"It's lovely." A bit impatiently, she shook off the weird vibe of safety the house conveyed and stepped onto a huge slab of sandstone and then onto the stone paved verandah. A group setting of wicker chairs were positioned further along beneath one of the windows giving the house a rustic and peaceful appeal.

Without bothering to knock, Rhiannon pushed open the unlocked door and walked into a large foyer. Tessa followed. Facing her was a long and wide hallway which she suspected ran the width of the house. Several openings and doors faced off on either side. Mid way down and a little beyond an arch positioned on plaster pillars set into the walls, a timber staircase flowed toward the upper level.

A cool breeze came out of nowhere and fluttered over Tessa's face. Then it was gone. Frowning, she glanced around the hallway.

As she had expected, the area was furnished with old and lovingly restored pieces, including an intricately carved hall stand that immediately captured her interest. The walls were painted a pale lemon and the architraves were highly polished red cedar. A faded tapestry mat covered part of the timber floor. Tessa rather suspected her entire apartment could fit inside the front entrance and hallway.

The mouth-watering smell of fried bacon and rich, dark coffee lingered in the air and Tessa's stomach rumbled.

Rhiannon paused and called, "Cooee!"

"We're in the kitchen," came floating back.

"This way." Rhiannon walked the length of the hall and disappeared through a door on her right.

Her heartbeat kicking up a gear at the sound of that voice, Tessa made a face and trotted along behind her. *Please, please don't let it be that crazy lady.* When she entered the large room she found her fears justified.

Seated around a long narrow table was the crazy lady from last night, her grandson eyeing Tessa coolly over the rim of his mug, the pregnant sergeant neat, if rather large, in her uniform, and another four old biddies with their avid stares all fixed in her direction.

Perfect. Just perfect.

She pinned a smile on her lips and said, "Good morning."

A chorus of greetings came back at her. A muffled growl came from the grey-muzzled, red kelpie curled in front of an old-fashioned wood stove and chowing noisily on a large bone.

"Easy Rufus," murmured the only guy present and the dog settled back to its breakfast. Dodge then took a sip of his drink before placing it with precision onto the table.

"There's a chair beside Dodge, Rhiannon," his grandmother piped up, indicating precisely where she meant with a wave of the toast she held in her hand. A blob of red jam plopped onto the table.

Dodge picked up his mug again and did his best to bury his face inside it.

Blushing, the nurse mumbled something, smiled and sat next to a sweet-looking old lady with soft, grey hair and wearing a pale pink cardigan.

Unperturbed, Dodge's cheeky grandmother said, "Guess it's up to you, Miss Gibson. Sit beside Dodge here, he doesn't bite."

"Much," inserted the police sergeant with a broad grin on her face. She forked a pile of bacon and scrambled eggs into her mouth and chewed with relish.

Not one to back down from a challenge, Tessa nodded, left her handbag and briefcase near the doorway and walked around the table.

The constable slid his chair along to make more room for her.

Politeness or maybe he wants to make sure not one spec of him will touch me. What does he think I am? Contaminated? Head held high and hating that the notion hurt, Tessa sat. Gripping the seat of her chair, she hopped it sideways until her thigh rested nicely along the length of his. Warmth from the heat of his body seeped through her jeans.

But he turned the tables on her. A shit-eating grin on his face, he placed a long arm over the back of her chair and leaned into her. Now she was all but cuddled up against his side.

His grandmother tilted back her head and burst into laughter.

Face burning, Tessa jerked away from him and fiddled with the silverware in front of her.

"I like a girl with balls." His grandmother extended a hand toward Tessa. "I'm Edwina Lette. And it's Ms, not Mrs. I never married."

A statement that made Tessa's head reel with questions she didn't dare ask...and were really none of her business anyway. For a long moment, Tessa hesitated remembering what had happened last night. Then, holding the older woman's gaze, she extended her hand. They shook and she got the strangest feeling they'd made a pact. Her tension fled when Edwina Lette simply winked and turned her attention back to her toast and jam.

"Thank you for the invitation. Everything smells delicious." Tessa picked up the latte-coloured linen napkin and placed it on her lap.

"Help yourself. We don't stand on ceremony here in Bindarra Creek," Dodge said, shoving a covered china bowl toward Tessa. "There's bacon, scrambled eggs, sausages, tomatoes, mushrooms and toast. I'd also try the strawberry and fig jam courtesy of Miss Collins. It's the best."

Tessa's mouth watered. She loved fried mushrooms on toast. At the end of the table, Miss Collins turned cherry red.

"We should introduce ourselves properly," Edwina said. "You've met my grandson and the midwife. Next to her is Beatrix Collins, her sister, Pamela Brown, our police sergeant Louise-Maree Baker and the woman in that dreadful orange dress is the rector's wife, Florence Miller. Next to her is Beth Roget, she owns the truck stop as you're coming into town. Esther Ainslie was supposed to be here but she bleated something about walking Rajah, that dog of hers. Now, you eat up while we fill you in."

"Gran," began Dodge.

His grandmother's chin jutted stubbornly. "You know she needs to hear from us the real deal about Bindarra Creek and not some hooey cow poop Donaldson chooses to spout."

Mrs Miller let loose a heavy sigh as she sugared her cup of tea. "I was hoping that Antonia would join us. Did you invite her, Edwina?"

"'Course I did." She sounded quite indignant. "But you know what she's like. Poor woman shuns company." Edwina leaned close to Tessa and waggled her eyebrows in a suggestive fashion.

"Uh huh." Nodding to show she was listening although really she had no idea what the old woman was on about, Tessa spooned fried tomatoes and onions onto her plate. She couldn't remember the last time she had a breakfast like this and she intended to make the most of it. Apparently, everyone else had the same idea as they returned to their meals.

The sun peeped through the large windows, casting a pale golden light over the timber cupboards and cream-painted walls. The friendly wash of chatter ebbed and flowed. Since it didn't appear Ms Lette intended to enliven the meeting with her parlour tricks, Tessa allowed her tense shoulders to relax, enjoying the warmth of the kitchen that wrapped around her like a blanket.

Dodge placed a glass jar with a cork topper to the left of her plate. "Here, sprinkle a pinch of basil over your tomatoes. All fresh from our garden."

He sounded like an expert. Tessa looked at her food then stared at him. Their gazes meshed and held. His clear eyes were more green than hazel today and were dappled like shadows playing over the surface of a stream. The corners of his mouth had deepened as if he held in a smile.

Pressure built inside her, hot and boiling. Her thigh muscles quivered from the effort to remain still and not flee.

Then he blinked. The heat in his eyes cooled to mirror the frosty dew-covered grass outside making her wonder whether she'd imagined the taut connection that had sizzled between them. Fingers shaking, she looked down at her plate. Her appetite had vanished.

"How many of these grants have you worked on, Miss Gibson?" Dodge took a slice of toast from the platter in front of him and crunched on the corner.

She could feel his eyes on her profile, weighing her up, ready to judge her response, ready to pounce at the first slip-up she made. Inwardly applauding her composure, she speared a mushroom and lied, "Three over the past four months." *Actually, your town is the only one.*

"That's fast."

"I don't believe in wasting time."

"And were all those grants approved?"

The other people seated around the table fell silent. The tense expectancy vibrating in the air was almost palpable.

Tessa lifted her head and said glibly, "Of course. This is what I do."

The collective gush of relief flowed into an excited outburst of chatter that filled the room like a party.

"Impressive," Dodge drawled.

Lifting her chin, Tessa meet his considering stare. "I know."

"And confident. I don't know whether to be in awe of you or terrified." His words were ripe with sarcasm and heat scalded Tessa's cheeks.

"You can be whatever you damn well like," she snapped, aware the pregnant sergeant had ceased her conversation with the midwife and now stared down the table toward her. What was with them anyway? Last night, Tessa had gained an impression of a strong bond between them. The comradeship of work partners or could it be something else? So far, no one had mentioned who the father of the baby was.

Small towns.

Such a small pool of possibilities.

Dodge grinned, revealing twin dimples and looked smug as if he'd achieved whatever he'd set out to do; as if he'd won. Tessa strongly suspected his motive was to get a rise out of her. But why? Was he hoping to flush the truth from her? There'd been a hint of suspicion in his even tones that she'd recognised. Had she somehow given herself away? *I knew he'd be a problem, I just knew it.*

"What do you get out of these proposals?"

"A commission, which the government includes in the grant payout," she said smoothly.

His eyebrows rose. "And what exactly did you do before this new scheme?"

His grandmother snorted. "Really, Dodge. Stop interrogating the girl as if she's a criminal."

Tessa dropped her fork then picked it up hoping he hadn't noticed her trembling hand.

"I'm doing my job, protecting this town." Dodge munched the rest of his toast, eyes still cool and fixed on Tessa.

"It's good that the town has someone so diligent looking out for them. I worked in another government department, now I freelance," she said.

"Yeah, you mentioned something about statistics."

The guy had the memory of an elephant, or a typical good cop. "That's right." Holding his gaze, she forked fragrant mushroom into her mouth and chewed. Then, the flavour exploded on her taste buds. "Oh my! This is wonderful."

"My specialty, although I'm famous for my pumpkin, almond mousse with whipped chocolate cream. I could give you a private tasting if you're keen."

Oh God! Did he mean...? No, surely not. Especially as the room was full of women, who would no doubt prove to be the biggest gossips the town boasted. And that didn't include his grandmother who sat a mere metre away with her beady gaze fixed on the pair of them. *I'm imagining things, get a grip.*

Her forehead felt damp and sweaty but hopefully hidden by the fall of her long fringe. She willed herself to remain calm and concentrate on the other questions she knew he wanted to fire away at her. *He's a cop, doing his job.* Common sense dictated there'd be a certain amount of suspicion she'd need to field.

"You're very defensive," Lou said in a sharp tone.

Tessa shrugged. "I've got a thing about sarcastic guys."

Everyone laughed including Dodge and the pregnant sergeant but her frown told Tessa she wasn't so easily convinced. The glance Lou sent Dodge was unfathomable making Tessa wonder again, just what their relationship was. If Lou had feelings for the constable, then Tessa would eat her woollen beanie if he returned them.

She finished the last of the creamy scrambled eggs and sighed. "That was exactly what I needed, thank you."

"Oh, the pleasure is all ours, Miss Gibson. You have no idea what your presence here means to us," Miss Collins said, a sweetly innocent smile spreading over her gentle features.

The food Tessa had just eaten curdled in her stomach like sour milk. She nodded and fiddled with the cutlery.

"Exactly," cut in her older sister, apparently anxious not to be outdone.

Mrs Miller clasped her hands together in a gesture Tessa was beginning to recognize as a favourite habit. "Our church."

"Don't start rabbiting on again about that blasted church, Florrie. We'll get to it but not now." Edwina Lette swept her gimlet gaze around the table and everyone immediately straightened.

It was like being addressed by a sergeant major thought Tessa feeling her back stiffen too. The elderly woman certainly had a presence and it was more than her stubborn streak. She possessed charm and charisma brimming with the mischief that glinted in her eyes.

"Let's get this meeting off the ground if you've all finished feeding your faces."

"Oh Edwina, I wish you wouldn't talk like that," wailed the rector's wife. "Shouldn't we give thanks?"

"Not now, Florrie. Time's awasting. It's like this Miss Gibson," began Edwina popping another slice of toast onto her plate and briskly buttering it to the edges.

"Call me Tessa, please."

Miss Collins murmured, "Tessa...such a lovely name."

"Tessa then. Beatrix, your jam is excellent as always." Dodge's grandmother locked her crystal sharp eyes onto Tessa's face. "Now...we need this money but not for any tom-fool idea of Barry Donaldson's. He's probably got some idiotic idea of building a race course or some such nonsense. The CWA members have drawn up a list of what needs doing to this town." She added a slice of ham to her toast and took a large mouthful that caused her cheeks to bulge like a guinea pig as she chewed.

"Lists are good," inserted Tessa. She loved lists herself.

Edwina swallowed. "Don't interrupt, I haven't finished."

Dodge chuckled, a deep sound that sent every nerve end Tessa possessed into frantic fluttering. "You'll soon learn if you stay here long enough, that my gran is a law unto her own."

Pride resonated in his voice and Tessa couldn't blame him. What would it be like to have someone like his grandmother in your life?

Beth Somebody-or-other, who wore an apron with a bib over a tight purple dress and had blonde hair to rival Dolly Parton, said loudly, "Business."

"Yes and no." Edwina polished off the last of her toast while everyone remained respectfully silent. Wiping her hands on her napkin, she continued. "In its heyday, Bindarra Creek boasted a population of almost ten thousand people including those who lived on the properties in our area. You wouldn't have recognized this place. It was a hub of activity, businesses thrived and our people were well-off. Now, our population is two thousand and seventy nine and dropping. There are many who struggle to make ends meet."

Around the table, everyone nodded. No trace of any smiles now.

Oh God. Please don't go on. I don't want to know. Tessa attempted to close her mind to the older woman's voice but the bleak words still penetrated, burrowing deep down into her conscience where they began to fester, like an abscess.

"We look after our own here, Tessa. We've a good barter system going for the staples in life, like vegetables, bread and fruit but people don't want charity." She paused as if gathering her thoughts.

"Most of our population are elderly with only the pension to pay their bills. And there are many who are old but don't meet the pension age requirements. There's pitifully few jobs here to sustain them. I'm sure you're well aware of all of this, judging from your speech last night."

"Yes," Tessa cut in, desperate to turn the tide of the conversation. "You mentioned you had a list? Sorry, but I mustn't be late for my meeting with the mayor."

"And of course, we wouldn't want to keep the mayor waiting," drawled Dodge.

For some odd reason, heat flooded Tessa's face.

"Pam? The list?" Edwina said.

"I have it here." Mrs Brown rose from her chair, walked in a stately fashion around the table and slapped two sheets of hand-written note paper down in front of Tessa. She remained hovering behind Tessa's chair like a vulture over road-kill. It gave Tessa the willies.

"Yes, well, I'll take a good look at it and do my best to incorporate your concerns into the proposal." Tessa fingered the pages.

"I know you will." Edwina Lette covered Tessa's restless hand with her own.

Looking up, she met the older woman's serious gaze and wondered at the sudden scald of tears behind her eyes. *I'm becoming weak. Think of the bigger picture. Think of Kaylee.* She withdrew her hand out from under Edwina's and lifted her chin. Was it her imagination or did disappointment wash over the other woman's face?

She pushed her plate away and made to stand.

Instantly, Dodge rose and stepped behind her to ease out her chair. His fingers brushed against her skin, just above where the collar of her jumper finished at her neck. Her flesh heated, a tingle radiating down her spine.

Murmuring a vague 'thank you' in general, she scooped up the list and hurried across the room to retrieve her bag and briefcase.

Rhiannon walked past her into the hall, saying, "I'll drop you back at the motel before I head to Doctor Warner's surgery."

"Oh and Tessa..." called Edwina.

Bracing herself, Tessa turned around to find everyone looking at her. Dodge had a pile of dirty dishes clasped in his hands and the memory of that brief contact liquefied her belly. His unsmiling, serious gaze unsettled her more than she cared to admit.

"If you've got ideas on how to attract more people into the town, we'd appreciate any help you can give us."

"Yes, bless you child," piped up Mrs Miller.

A chorus of 'thank you's' followed Tessa every dragging step she took down that long hallway and out the door of Fig Tree Lodge.

CHAPTER FOUR

Dodge unlocked the twelve centimetre-thick plank door of the old police station and pushed inside. Behind him, Lou could be heard scrapping her boots on the straw mat on the doorstep.

When she finally stepped onto the old linoleum-covered floor, she said, "You've carted in mud."

"I'll fix it, later." He stalked past the battered counter that had stood the test of time ever since the station had been remodelled from the original clay brick and asbestos tiles structure of 1885 in 1912 to Besser brick and iron. Drawing out his chair, he sat and pulled the keyboard toward him.

"I'll get the fire going. This place is freezing," Lou said.

Dodge bit back his sigh and shoved to his feet again. "Sit down, Lou. You're in no condition to be carting wood about."

"And you're in a pisser of a mood. What's wrong with you?"

When he glanced over, he found her glaring at him, her hands planted on her wide hips. Unable to voice his conflicting thoughts, he paced to and fro from the stack of wood near the door then over to the fireplace on the opposite wall, before crouching down to build the fire. Once he had the blaze going, he straightened and faced her, feeling a bit like she was the firing squad.

She hadn't moved.

And looked like she was going nowhere fast until she'd had her answers.

"It's Tessa, isn't it? You think there's something sus about her?"

"There's a lot riding on this grant. A lot of people will be very disappointed if it falls through."

"Tell me something I don't know." Rolling her eyes, Lou allowed her hands to fall to her sides and wandered behind the counter to sift through the small stack of mail.

Dodge stared at her, uncertain how much to confess. Shit, he didn't even know himself what to confess. "I thought I'd get a background check done on her," he admitted slowly.

Lou looked up, surprise etched on her face. "Wow, you really are rattled."

"Totally off the books, of course." Dodge began to sweat, even though the air was still cold enough to rival a refrigerator.

"Of course," echoed Lou in a wondering tone.

Feeling pressured to explain, he rushed into speech. "Look, it's not that I've got anything to go on but I'd like to make sure she's on the up and up."

"You can't deny the government's 'Rebuild our Towns' scheme isn't legit." She slit open an envelope and began to read its contents.

"I know." He knew he sounded frustrated but he couldn't help it. Something about Tessa Gibson was off and he wished like hell, he could put his finger on whatever it was that had aroused his suspicions.

"Look, Dodge." Lou placed the letter on the counter and stared at him. "You sure this is your cop instinct at work and not some guy thing?"

His jaw clenched, he wheeled his chair closer to his desk. Hunching his shoulders as if that would be sufficient to ward off any further acute observations from his sergeant, he did his best to ignore her.

But she just kept on swinging like the last batsman at a one-day cricket match. Heaven help the guy she eventually decided to commit to because, bloody hell, she was one determined woman.

"Your complete silence on the subject confirms it. You like her."

"I'm not blind," he defended himself.

Lou chuckled. "It's good to see that you're in full functioning order. I must admit, I was beginning to wonder."

"Bloody hell, you've been talking to Gran."

"Mmm, more like listening." Papers rustled as she worked her way through their correspondence. "She worries about you."

"She shouldn't, I'm doing okay."

"Yeah right, living the life of a monk. A guy your age should be out partying, meeting girls, settling down."

"I happen to like my life exactly the way it is."

"Hence your reluctance to ask Rhiannon Scott out."

"Haven't you got work to do?" He indicated the mail.

Lou grimaced. "Not much here besides one bill and some junk mail."

"You're not one to talk."

"Whatdoyamean?"

"That baby of yours. You intend to make an honest man out of some guy? Who is he anyway?" He grinned.

"None of your beeswax." She laughed back at him.

"I think I can make a good guess."

The smile fell from Lou's face and she stared toward the door. Dodge wondered what she was thinking about and added, "Have you told him?"

She started riffling through the envelopes again as if her life depended on it. "Of course I have."

"That would explain the sudden way he took off about four months ago," Dodge said drily.

"You know who he is, don't you?"

"Yeah. I'm not blind. I could see you and my dear old dad had sparks flying." He prodded the fire. "I could talk to him."

"Crap no. Please don't. If he doesn't want anything to do with me and the baby, that's his call. I don't need a bloke to hold my hand."

Dodge met Lou's anxious gaze. "No matter what happens between you two, I'm here for you."

She nodded, her eyes suspiciously bright.

He winked. "You know half the town thinks I'm the father."

Lou sniggered and, glad her brief sadness had passed, Dodge grinned back.

"Nothing like being fodder for the gossips. Now, we were talking about you."

"Dammit."

"I think your gran is rubbing off on me. That has to be the reason I'm worried about your love life."

"Heaven help us all."

Lou balled up a piece of paper and tossed it across the room, hitting him on the head. "Take that. So come on, fess up. You gonna make a move on this Gibson chick?"

"I just told you...I like my life just fine." Smile fading, Dodge scooped the wad of paper off the floor and chucked into the bin beside his desk.

"Pity. I'd enjoy watching the fireworks from the sideline. Although..." Lou paused.

Annoyed but unable to stop himself, he glanced over. Lou was staring up at the ceiling, her right hand doing that soothing round and round thing she did constantly these days on her swollen belly.

She muttered, "You know, I'm fairly certain this post traumatic thing I did at that course in Armidale last year, touched on residue paranoia."

"What?"

"Your partner's trial. Sorry, ex-work partner. It must be hard, watching her being put through the wringer and her life exposed for everyone to wonder over. I guess you must be feeling a certain amount of guilt that she was charged with theft, tampering with evidence and dereliction of duty." Lou stopped looking at the ceiling and pointed at him.

"Based on your evidence, you know they'll probably throw the book at her. She'll be lucky to be out in twenty years." She sighed.

"I'm worried about you Dodge. This could explain your hypersensitivity to anything out of the ordinary. You know, your paranoia to suspect every stranger that comes to town," she concluded in a sympathetic tone.

"We don't get that many people coming to Bindarra Creek," Dodge deflected wryly. His gut was roiling, acidic bile clogged his throat and he swallowed hard.

"Too true. You know what I think, don't you?"

"Yeah, you've made that obvious on a number of occasions, Lou." He ran a hand through his hair. "Go on then, get it off your chest."

"Think about the counselling sessions the nobs offered you. It may help to ease your fear of making another mistake."

"I didn't make any mistakes," he all but snarled. "The inquiry cleared me of any complicity."

"Hey, keep your hair on! I'm sorry. That came out all wrong. I know all that, geez I'm not accusing you of anything, Dodge."

"Then you'd be the first." Grinding his molars together so fiercely that pain shot along his jaw and locked his muscles, he glanced down at where he'd fisted his hands on the desk, remembering - the side-long glances of his so-called mates, the whispers and glares that followed him wherever he went, like the spectre of death.

No-one wanted to partner with him.

No-one trusted him.

And even now, eighteen months after the event, he still hadn't worked out whether it was because they suspected he'd been involved or whether they thought he'd grass them out too at the first opportunity.

If it hadn't been for his barrister uncle, he could well be sitting in the cell next to his ex-partner of four years, Sara Pyeon.

The whole mess had signalled the end of his career as a copper, one that he'd worked his arse off at school for, one that he'd thought was his calling. His superintendent had all but told him to his face he needed to lay low for a while, probably for a long, long while – cops never forgot. But he'd believed what he'd done had been the right course of action. He still did. Apparently, he'd been the only one to think that, so he'd requested and been given, a transfer to the town where he'd spent the first twelve years of his life.

Bindarra Creek.

A town so small, the majority of Australia had never heard of it.

And probably never would.

He stared moodily at the screen where a message telling him to key in his password, blinked on and on and on.

Sara had begged him to keep quiet. To give her a chance to pay it all back. To help her. He *had* hesitated, he hadn't dobbed her in straight away. Instead he'd gone home to his one bedroom apartment in Coogee to think.

But she'd been seen.

And the next thing, Dodge knew he'd been hauled in and was fronting the head of his department and being bombarded with words like, full inquiry, Royal Commission, dirty cops, and so on and so forth. He'd been fingered as well. Desperate to clear his own name, it had all come out. And Sara had been charged and fired from the job she'd loved. Uncertain as to how deeply he'd been involved, they'd given him an official warning, his pristine record marred with a question mark.

He hadn't spoken to Sara since. In fact, he'd been warned not to or the evidence and the trial could be jeopardised.

A mug of coffee was plonked onto the desk and Lou nudged his shoulder with her elbow.

"Drink up," she said gruffly.

The rich aroma hit his nostrils and he sniffed it in, feeling a little of his tension ebb at her peace offering. "I don't believe I'm over-reacting."

"You're right then, it won't hurt to check Gibson out. Go-on, I'll deal with the paperwork for that broken window on Tuesday, if you like."

"Thanks, Lou." He looked up and smiled.

By the way she grinned back at him, he knew their friendship was back on an even keel. He gulped a hot mouthful, enjoying the hit of caffeine, then reached for the mouse.

***

Tessa leaned back in her chair, her hands neatly clasped in her lap and listened while Mayor Donaldson rambled on with what sounded to her, like a whole pile of... *what had Edwina Lette called it? Oh yes, hooey cow poop*.

A bubble of laughter rose and Tessa had to bite down hard not to allow it to escape. Surreptitiously she glanced over at the small, old mantle clock ticking away above an empty fireplace and checked the time. For one hour and fifteen minutes she'd been trapped in this meeting and there was no sign of it ending any time soon.

Her nose twitched as she attempted not to breathe in the odour of dampness, the mustiness of mouse droppings and something she rather thought might be boiled cabbage. Thank heavens, she'd been spared having to eat breakfast here. The wife part of the team who owned and ran the motel was lovely if a bit harassed, rushing in and out of the small dining room with a jug of cold water with bits of lemon bobbing about in it and a plate of stale arrowroot biscuits. Tessa would have preferred a working urn and some tea bags.

She winced at the limp-green painted walls and the hardness of the vinyl and metal chair under her. But the view of the countryside was arresting.

Allowing her mind to drift, she stared out the double glass sliding door that led to the side garden. Her gaze traced the distant outlines of the rolling hills to the east of the town and that she'd learned today were the western slopes of the Great Dividing Range. Somewhere along the road that wound past the McLean's motel was a fascinating place called, Akuna National Park. Mayor Donaldson had mentioned how it was famous for its natural waterfalls, rock pools and lush flora. Although, if truth be told, Tessa had never heard of it.

If Kaylee was here, we could make a day of it, maybe camp overnight. That sounded like fun and Kaylee would love it. *Who am I kidding? I've never camped in my life.* But for the first time, the idea sounded tempting. Her amused snort stopped the mayor mid-sentence and he looked over at her, eyebrows raised.

"Hay fever," she said, then gathering her thoughts added quickly, "I completely understand your concerns. However the process is fairly streamlined."

"Oh I'm positive you'll steer us through whatever red-tape is necessary." Beaming, he leaned over and patted her arm. "As I was saying, about the specifics of the proposal..."

Tessa nodded as if in complete agreement and raising her voice cut in, "The race course is a great idea." Amazing how on track that woman had been, predicting the mayor's fixation. "However, if we're going to push this grant over the finishing line, we're going to have to appeal to the base roots of the government's initiative. That means, the race course is off the list."

"Absolutely out of the question!" declared Donaldson, his face infused like an overripe tomato. The other six men at the rectangular table glanced at each other and let him rant.

Talk about being out numbered!

"Please, let me finish." Tessa held up a hand and he subsided, scowling. "Don't forget you will need to account for all the money you receive and there'll be an official government inspection of your records. It's possible if you stick to the core aspects of your proposal and are careful with budget constraints there may be funds leftover."

"Do you really think so, Miss Gibson?"

Wow, he's dead set on getting this race track up and running. I wonder why? "I'm sorry mayor but you need to do this by the book." Another excruciating thirty minutes of blustering and grumbling and finally, Tessa was able to wave the mayor, two aging councilmen and a big property owner he'd brought along with him for moral support, out the door leaving behind the solicitor and another local bigwig.

Slumping back in her chair, Tessa mused, "I could kill for a hot cuppa."

"What I wouldn't give for a decent coffee but the staff here have no idea. Burn the beans every time without fail. There is no excuse for incompetence," said Gordon Fairfax, who appeared to be as full of his own importance as the mayor.

A heavy pressure built behind her eyes, signalling a major headache was on the way. Tessa shut down her tablet where she'd been making notes and said, "I'm surprised none of the CWA committee were here to put forward their suggestions."

Clarence Lansky, a solicitor in his late forties and who Tessa had liked immediately, ran a finger over his moustache and grinned. "Banned."

Tessa laughed then sobered. "I'm not surprised. They're quite a determined bunch. But I don't blame them and the items on their list are more in keeping with what the government hopes to achieve."

"I couldn't agree more." Mr Lansky gazed at her with approval. "Now, young lady, I understand you'll need a small, quiet office with wifi access and I have just the place for you."

"Thank you." She stood. "If you don't mind showing me now, I'd love to get started."

The two men rose to their feet, Lansky with an old-world courtesy, the other reluctantly.

Fairfax stated, "I appreciate good workers."

Uncertain as to exactly what the devil he was talking about, Tessa extended her hand to his and they shook.

She said smoothly, "No doubt we'll meet again, Mr Fairfax."

The solicitor slid his hand under her elbow and after picking up her briefcase ushered her out of the motel, calling out a cheery Thanks for everything' to the unseen McLeans as they walked to his car.

CHAPTER FIVE

By mid-morning the next day, Tessa had the draft proposal neatly outlined and had started on fleshing out the details. At this rate, she anticipated this first stage should be finished around 3pm. Then a quick text to the mayor to organize another meeting for his final approval. And after that, the transfer of the agreed information onto the official application form which required his signature before submission.

Tomorrow night...I should have the grant lodged by tomorrow night. Tapping her pen on the desk, she stared out the window of her borrowed office.

Outside, an icy wind whipped down the street, scattering leaves and a few scraps of litter along the pavement. It was overcast. The heavy fog that had shrouded the world when Tessa had emerged from her motel room this morning had yet to fully dissipate. The greyness and the chill factor served to weigh down her spirits as she'd worked through the past three hours on the proposal.

Such a stark contrast to how her day had begun yesterday. The frosty fields and the thin, golden rays of the sun. That amazing breakfast and the surprising feeling of companionship she'd experienced at Fig Tree Lodge. The heat and interest she'd seen in Dodge's eyes.

Today, it was as if those few warm moments had never happened.

Today, she was alone in a cavernous concrete-block building with its large uncurtained windows facing the street, cracked linoleum covered floors and pitifully few radiators to ward off the chill. Long and narrow it squatted on its allotment like a box and was just about as attractive. It consisted of one main room partitioned off with free-standing acoustic screens into four separate work areas, a tiny kitchenette at the rear that led to a cramped toilet and washroom. In each square was a basic desk and computer chair and there was a row of locked filing cabinets along one wall.

She'd learned yesterday, the solicitor rented the entire building even though he worked in Bindarra Creek one out of five working days. Tessa assumed on the days when he wasn't in town, the building stood empty apart from an administration assistant who apparently appeared for one hour every morning to check the mail. Mr Lansky was but one of a few visiting professionals who divided their working week between a number of small isolated towns and villages in the area. Most of them, however, lived in either Moree or Armidale. But Mr Lansky lived right here in Bindarra Creek. Perhaps that also gave him another reason to be an enthusiastic, devotee of the need to bring life and prosperity back to this area.

What a pity, none of it would ever happen.

An elderly grey-haired lady passed by the window, peering into the shadowy office. Tessa recognized her as the sweet Miss Collins and, smiling, lifted a hand in greeting. But Miss Collins turned away and hunching her back against the wind struggled down the street. An old-fashioned string bag bulging with zucchinis and cabbages hung from her arm and banged against her leg with each step she took.

Tessa frowned. Hang on. Wasn't the old lady wearing the same outfit she'd worn yesterday? Her raggedy cardigan and patched trousers looked no match for the bitterness of the frosty winter morning. Didn't she possess a coat of some sort?

The urge to rush out the door and take her burden away was strong.

Not my problem, Tessa chanted fiercely.

Miss Collins disappeared from sight but not from Tessa's mind. In her imagination she saw the old lady trudging up the road, shoulders slumped, the wind cutting through her thin clothes freezing her old bones, her face and hands red and chafed from the cold.

A shiver prickled Tessa's flesh. She pulled the collar of her ruby-red, woollen jumper up higher over her neck, huddling down into its warmth. Her hand trembled as she minimised the spreadsheet and stared with burning eyes at her screen save.

A white Californian-style bungalow nestled amidst several groupings of Christmas Palm Trees, King Palms and Lipstick Palm trees together with bamboo clumpings, all set against a back-drop of brilliant blue sky.

This was it. This was her goal. Her dream. A little house in Darwin and new names for both of them.

"Nice pic."

The male voice coming from close behind caused her to jump in her seat. Pulse skittering out of control, she whirled around and found Dodge looking over her shoulder at her laptop.

"How did you get in here?"

He shrugged his lovely wide shoulders made bulky by the thick navy-blue jacket he wore over his uniform. "Rear door."

"Seriously? Wasn't it locked?" Her voice came out shriller than she wanted and she saw his eyes narrow and switch to examine her face. The emerald-green shade of his beanie he'd pulled down over his ears was reflected in his eyes. They looked like dark, mysterious pools with specks of gold dust glittering in the depths. He raised one eyebrow and it struck her she'd been gaping like some star-struck teenager.

"We've got keys to the major buildings in town. In case of emergencies. You sound awfully nervous. Something wrong?" he drawled.

Tessa pulled herself together. "No. No. You gave me a fright, sneaking up on me like that," she accused, swiveling back around and quickly closing her laptop.

"You're acting very furtive. Maybe there's something on that computer of yours you don't want me to see."

Teeth clenched, Tessa immediately flung open her laptop. "See? There's nothing here. And if you've come to check up on me, here's where I'm up to so far." She clicked the spreadsheet open.

"You sure are feisty. Must be all that red in your brown hair." He touched her single braid lying over her shoulder.

"I don't like being spied on."

"Hey." He held up his hands. "I'm not spying." He gave a sudden boyish grin. "Okay, maybe just a little. I'm like everyone else in this town, keen to see the proposal go through. I wanted to know if you had everything you need."

"I can understand that," Tessa said slowly, an image of Miss Collins walking past flashed into her mind. "People are struggling here, aren't they?"

"Yeah." His voice serious, the constable stepped forward and perched on the edge of her desk.

This close, Tessa had a nice view of how the material of his pants stretched across his muscled thighs. Why was she noticing so much about this guy? Normally, she was oblivious. Straightening her spine, she jerked her gaze back to her screen. She mumbled huskily, "Here is what I've done so far. I should be finished the draft by this afternoon and intend to fire it off tomorrow night after Mayor Donaldson signs on the dotted line."

"That soon?" He peered at the spreadsheet.

"I don't see any reason for delay, do you?"

"No, I guess not. Makes you sound as if you can't wait to get out of here though." There he was, back to his probing cop-like questions.

Hoping he couldn't read her guilty intentions on her face, Tessa said, "The sooner I'm finished, the quicker you'll see the results." *Not if I have anything to do with it.* Miss Collins timid smile rose in her mind. Furious with herself, Tessa thrust the thought away.

"I can't argue with that." He rose to his feet.

Tessa stared at her laptop feeling the heat of his presence as if he was plastered right up against her body. Her skin tightened as her heartbeat kicked up a gear. *Maybe I've got a virus.* That could explain how hot she felt. There was no way she intended to entertain any other possibility.

"You didn't answer my question." He waited until she dragged her reluctant gaze up to his face.

The moment their eyes met, a quiver ran through her body and she had to swallow.

"Need anything, Tessa?" He spoke the words soft and deep. His eyes seemed to search her soul and she shook inside.

"I'm fine, if a little cold," she croaked.

"Yeah, these Besser-block offices are difficult to heat. You should be here once summer hits. In the older buildings, we boil like lobsters." He grinned.

She smiled back and had to hold in her gasp at the sudden hot glitter in his eyes.

"I know just the thing to warm you up."

Oh gosh, did he mean...? Her pulse skyrocketed and all the moisture in her mouth fled.

"Coffee or a hot cuppa? Maybe some raisin toast or a slice of hot, buttered, banana bread? Come on. I know just the place." He held out his hand about a centimeter from her nose.

Cursing herself for her stupid thoughts, she stuttered a 'no thanks'.

"I'm not taking no for an answer. You've been working long enough and need a break." He waggled his fingers.

Wordlessly, she gave him her hand and allowed him to pull her to her feet. Too late, she realised she now stood in his personal space, the solid wall of his chest about two centimetres from her body. What would it be like to lay her head against his warm skin and listen to the steady beat of his heart as he wrapped his strong arms around her?

Feeling close to dumb tears, she hastily stepped back. Her boots tangled with the chair leg and she tipped backwards.

"Woah!" His hands gripped her waist and hauled her flush against him, exactly where she'd been daydreaming about a second ago.

"Sorry. Sorry." She pulled out of his hold with the force of a rocket. This time avoiding colliding with her chair.

Her face on fire, she bent over her desk, did another save of her work and shut down her computer. "There. I'm ready, Constable Myers." She looped the straps of her large handbag over her arm and stood, head held high, aiming for cool and composed.

"Dodge, please or Dylan, but I'm only called that by my grandmother and her cronies when

I'm in trouble. We'll go out the front. I locked the back door behind me when I came inside." Dodge led the way to the entrance where he held the door open for her to step through. He touched her briefly on her elbow. "Watch those steps, they're slippery when wet."

She knew his manners were impeccable with everyone and yet she couldn't help feeling as if he considered her someone precious.

Focus. Focus. Focus.

The wind slammed into her and almost sent her reeling. Really, it was a wonder poor Miss Collins hadn't been knocked off her feet. Her respect grew for the uncomplaining old lady. Yanking out a pair of woollen gloves from her handbag, she pulled them over her tingling fingers. Next, she found her beanie and hauled it over her head. "Where are we going?"

"How about a stroll around town? Then we'll go home for that hot drink and a bite to eat."

Was he mad? A stroll around town in this gale?

Already shivering, she hopped from one foot to the other while he closed the door and stepped off the porch onto the pavement beside her.

"It feels like it's about to snow." Dubiously, Tessa stared at the threatening clouds and hugged her waist.

"Nah. It'll probably lift in the arvo. If we're lucky the wind will drop too." He held his chin high and sniffed the air. His eyes sparkled as he gazed at her. "Walking will get your blood flowing and warm you up."

"If you say so." Although Tessa could think of far better ways to get warm, like curling up in front of a fire snug under a rug – anywhere would do, as long as it was out of this howling wind.

Dodge chuckled. In a casual manner, he flung an arm about her shoulder and hugged her close as they set off down the street. He walked fast in a long-legged stride which Tessa found she could match. He was right. They'd barely covered a few paces and even though the wind hadn't abated she was warmer. She rolled her eyes. How annoying.

As they strode along, he pointed out items of interest and touched on the history of some of the buildings. She found herself engrossed, not just in listening to the sound of his voice but also learning of the lives of the people who'd come before them. She hadn't expected the town to be so old with a mixture of late 1900's structures mixed with a few 1950's buildings. Some were double stories and some single. Others were made from old brick and had iron roofs, a few such as the solicitor's office were made from Besser-blocks and a couple were timber or weatherboard clad with old roof tiles. Dodge told her that there were three shanty-type houses in town that dated back to pre-1842 when the place had been little more than a staging post to rest horses and bullock teams on their way to and from Armidale and Moree.

The solicitor's building where she'd been working was situated on a corner block. Opposite was a second-hand bookshop with a vacant lot on the right hand side and a narrow alley way on the left. The lure of passing through the timber door into the depths of the book shop was strong. Its two full-length bow windows were crammed with faded, leather-bound books and Tessa fairly itched to riffle through the shelves.

But she resisted. This wasn't a holiday. She was here to work.

What appeared to be living quarters occupied the second floor of the bookshop. Running alongside the alley was the fairly modern-looking chemist next to another narrow-width, double-story building housing an antique shop with dusty, grimy windows.

Their quick steps took them past the dress shop next door to the solicitor's office then a hairdressers with double-glass doors. The timber surrounds painted crimson-red had a large placard attached saying 'Open'. The twin, large plate-glass windows gave a glimpse into what appeared to be the only busy shop in town. Three women sat in chairs while another two clad in matching powder-pink tracksuits bustled about the room.

"My gran works there when she's got bookings," Dodge indicated the hairdressers.

"A hairdresser?" Now that was surprising.

Dodge laughed. "Far from it. She rents a small room where she reads people's palms and tea leaves and offers a whole pile of advice people usually don't want to hear. See that doorway on the left with the bead curtain?"

Tessa giggled.

He leaned closer to her ear. "She brews her best spells there."

At that, she laughed and nudged him with her elbow.

"Hey, don't take my word for it. Ask anyone." The smile in his voice was downright infectious. "On the corner is Doc Warner's surgery, should you need him. He's a good bloke. Bit of a character though, so be warned."

"Everyone here seems to be a bit of a character," Tessa said wryly.

"Small towns, isolated communities. It happens. At least, we're not boring."

"Have you always lived here?"

His gaze lifted as if he sought the answer to her question in the grey clouds. "Dad and I left when I was twelve."

No mention of his mother and there'd been an inflection of pain in his voice that made Tessa hesitate to continue. Instead she asked the question that had been niggling away at her ever since they first met. "What brought you back? A girl? Someone special?" Holding her breath, she couldn't believe how much she wanted to hear his reply.

"That takeaway over there makes great hamburgers," he said, not answering the question. His arm slid from her shoulder as he pointed across the street. He made no attempt to repeat the friendly gesture. "And if you're after the best coffee in town, I'd recommend the Cyprus Café."

Tessa didn't feel so warm anymore.

They'd come to the end of the block and turned left onto Willow Tree Drive. The uneven pavement gave way to rough ground covered with weeds.

"I wanted a change," he finally answered abruptly.

Oooookaaaay. Obviously a touchy subject. And he was obviously lying through his teeth. What could he be hiding?

"Mrs Brown and her sister live in that house over there. You met them at breakfast the other morning. They're mad keen gardeners."

Tessa turned her head and inspected the house that looked to be one step away from being condemned. Her heart sank. Rusting iron roof that probably let water inside every time it rained, rotting weatherboard sidings, sagging picket fence with the majority of its palings missing, the gun-barrel designed building screamed fatigue and hardship. On the narrow front porch, was an ancient sofa currently occupied by three cats all sitting up and watching them pass by. The block was wide, had no driveway and appeared to stretch for some distance behind the house. The only saving features were the five mature fruit trees laden with their produce and that had been planted down one side of the block. The sunniest side, Tessa realized and buried her misgivings about the sisters' hard lives. Instead she turned her head and admired Dodge's home.

"We're here," announced Dodge as they stepped onto the gravel drive.

She admitted, "It's a lovely building." Their footsteps crunched loud as they approached the house.

"Fig Tree Lodge has been in our family for quite a few years now. Ernest Lette built it for his wife, Charlotte, back in 1889."

"Sounds like your family is part of Bindarra Creek history."

Dodge led the way to the back of the house. "On my mother's side, I guess we have been. They were originally from County Wexford in

Ireland and came to Australia in 1850. Anne and Peter Lette were their names and they were only eighteen. I think they moved here in 1856 but Gran would know more. Dad's lot come from Armidale and, way back were originally from England."

"They must have been very brave." Tessa frowned, thinking about that young Irish couple and how determined they must have been to make a new life for themselves in an unknown and largely unmapped country. To the best of her knowledge her mother had been an only child of elderly parents who'd wanted nothing to do with her. And Tessa's father could have been anyone. It both fascinated and made her envious of anyone who had history.

Who had a family.

They'd reached the kitchen door. This was the first time Tessa had had a chance to see the rear of the Lodge. A Queenslander room was in the process of being built along the full-width of the building. Another three ancient fig trees were planted well away from the house and past them, was a dilapidated convict brick building, several fruit trees and at least seven raised vegetable beds.

"Excuse the mess." Dodge picked up a large toolbox and moved it out of the way. "I did a bit of work this morning before fronting up at the cop shop."

Tessa remembered the furniture in the hall and wondered whether he'd had a hand in restoring some of those pieces. "You're a carpenter?"

"Haven't done any formal training. It's just something I'm interested in, plus this place desperately needs repairs or it'll fall down around Gran's ears. Here we go." After scraping his boots on the straw mat, he pushed open the door and stepped aside to allow her to enter first. Tessa hastily wiped her boots on the mat.

Once inside, Dodge slipped off his jacket and slung it over the back of a chair. "Take a seat." He waved her toward the table where a bowl of fruit resided and a centerpiece of intricately crocheted lace ran down the length.

"I'm not much of a cook but I can boil water. Please let me help."

"Okay then." Dodge busied himself by opening cupboards and retrieving mugs and plates while Tessa filled the jug with water from the tap. "You don't like cooking?"

"It's a necessary evil."

He laughed. "I love it. So does Lou. We like concocting recipes together."

"Really?" Something painful snapped at her heart. She could just imagine Dodge and Lou in this comfortable, warm kitchen, working together, smiling, bumping into each other...

Hastily, she shut down that direction of thought. "Where's your grandmother?"

"She could be anywhere but since Rufus isn't here, I'd say she's walked over to see one of her cronies."

Tessa turned the kettle on then leaned back against the counter watching Dodge set the table before picking up a cake tin and looking at her.

"Banana bread? Lou's recipe," he said, that curious half-smile playing around his supple lips.

It would be.

"Lovely," she said, through her teeth as he placed the tin on the table.

"Tea or coffee?"

"Tea, please."

Nodding, Dodge measured spoonfuls of leaves into a bone-china pot. "You can heat up the banana bread in the microwave if you don't mind."

"No worries."

Soon the room was filled with the rich scent of hot banana bread and fragrant tea.

Seated at the table, Tessa slathered her slice of bread with real butter and took a bite. Her momentary resentment toward the other woman melted much like the food in her mouth. "Your friend is wasted as a police sergeant. This is awesome."

Beside her, Dodge sipped his tea in silence.

She wondered what he was thinking. She hadn't failed to notice how his expression had turned from warm and friendly to deadpan after his mobile had pinged the moment before they'd sat down. He'd slipped his phone from his pocket and had turned his back while he read the text.

"We've got a problem," Dodge said now, placing his cup carefully back into its saucer.

Oh shit. Here we go. Maintaining her calm, she finished the remainder of her slice.

"I ran a police check on your background."

"Of course you did."

"You've got a sealed juvie record."

Fury rose masking her sharp disappointment. *This is it. What always happens, what never disappears no matter how hard I try to do the right thing.* Make one mistake and in the eyes of the law, you're tarred with it for the remainder of your life. And what a mistake – stealing a meat pie that first winter alone on the streets when she was so hungry she thought her ribs touched her spine. It had been hard, so hard to survive without descending further into crime but apart from begging a few times, she'd managed it.

Tessa closed her mind to the reason why she was here in this town. She couldn't afford to let that matter. What mattered was she'd been judged and found wanting based on her past. But she'd had so few choices back then. And nothing...nothing would ever make her go down the same road as her mother.

"You're not saying anything in your defense."

"What do you want me to say? You've made up your mind. I can see it in your face. I'm some kind of low-life crim." She'd learned a long time ago, attack was the best form of defense.

"It's a juvie record and I didn't break the seal," he said wryly. "Care to tell me what it contains?"

"Why don't you find out for yourself?"

"This attitude is not doing you any favours." His voice was mild but she wasn't fooled.

Tessa set her jaw and glowered. She could feel his eyes on her, studying her, waiting for the first crack to appear so he could pounce. Well, stuff him. She was tough. She'd had to be or she'd never have survived this long on her own.

"Come on, Tessa. This isn't personal. I'm only doing my job."

"I was young and stupid." Surely that would be enough to stop him asking any more questions?

"We can all make dumb mistakes," he said.

She shot him a quick look.

He was frowning and staring into his cup, as if, like his grandmother, he searched for answers in the dregs. "Your record has been clean since then."

It hadn't been much of a record anyway but she'd had to clean up her act. She had someone depending on her.

When she didn't respond, he sighed. "This is my job. It sucks sometimes but I take it seriously."

Duly warned and noted.

He added, "Anything else you need to tell me?"

Like how I'm intend to take the majority of the town's grant money and run for my life? Would that do? She could imagine the scorn on his face, the coldness in his eyes. The way his grandmother and her friends would turn their backs on her and for one long minute, she wished things could have been different. Tessa could feel his eyes on her profile. She wet her dry lips and made a desperate attempt to deflect him. "I have an eight year old daughter."

"Get out of here. You don't look old enough although I know from your driver's licence you're twenty four, almost four years younger than me."

The honest surprise in his voice had her turning to face him. Hopefully, that tricky moment had passed. She shrugged. "I did say I was young and stupid."

"You forgot honest." He smiled and laid his hand over hers where it rested on the table.

Geez, Dodge. If only you knew. Blinking rapidly, she wondered how to get herself out of this house. And away from him.

"No, Mr Gibson on the scene? No committed boyfriend?" He lifted his hand and slowly traced a fingertip up and down each of her fingers before feathering the merest brush of his knuckles over the back of her hand.

Goosebumps broke out over her skin. "You know the answer to that, says on my licence I'm single. Actually, I never married Kaylee's father." *I didn't have the chance. He would have married me. That stupid, stupid drag race. We were both so very young. Both so alone apart from each other. But Ian was more...he was reckless.*

"Just checking." Dodge gave a lop-sided grin that had her heart leap-frogging against her ribs. "Then you've got something in common with Gran."

Heaven forbid! She forced out the words. "About my record, what do you intend to tell everyone?"

Picking up the teapot, Dodge poured them both another cup. "It's a juvenile record. As long as you're clean now, I don't see how it's of any relevance."

If only you knew. But like a dog with a bone, she couldn't leave it alone. She had to goad him. "I can't believe you checked up on me." *And I can't believe his opinion matters so much.*

Frowning, he narrowed his eyes. "I explained that already."

Tessa pursed her lips, then almost leapt from the chair when his gaze lowered. And lingered. Fascinated, she watched as a flush flowed up from his neck above his collar and over his cheekbones.

"How about we call a truce? We leave the past in the past and concentrate on today," he said gruffly.

"Sounds like a good plan to me."

"But before we do, I have to ask one more question."

Her hand poised to pick up her cup, froze. *Dammit! Why couldn't he give it a rest?*

He cleared his throat. "Where's your parents? Why weren't they looking out for you?"

"Not everyone has the perfect family, constable." Knees knocking together under her jeans, she shoved to her feet. "Thanks for the break but I've got work to do." Her voice cracked.

Snatching up her handbag, she hurried across the room, slamming the door shut behind her.

CHAPTER SIX

Back at the solicitor's office, Tessa worked like a fiend for the remainder of the day. At every creak of the building or moan of the wind, she'd jump up and spin around, half expecting to see Dodge standing there but no one entered the office.

No one called. No text messages inviting her to dinner or breakfast. No one walked along the street in front of the window.

She could have been the only soul left on the planet.

Every ten minutes or so, she'd flick on her mobile and stare at the photo of Kaylee she'd taken last year before her operation. A potent reminder of what was at stake.

I can do this – I have to. Kaylee is my family. She's all I need.

Her fingers flew over the keys and she had the draft proposal finished half an hour before her self-imposed deadline. But it took the next thirty minutes anyway to finally get hold of Mayor

Donaldson who promptly advised her to email the proposal. He ended the conversation with an 'I'll get back to you tomorrow' and hung up before she could protest.

Glaring at her mobile, she sagged back into the chair. Her shoulders and back ached. She'd have to do some serious stretching to work out those kinks or she'd never sleep well later. Opening her email account, she soon had the necessary correspondence sent off. She shut down her computer then packed her few belongings into her laptop case with a kind of grim precision.

A queer sensation, rather like desperation scratching away inside her head. That little voice that had stood her in such good stead in her past, kept telling her, *leave – go now – before it's too late.*

But why? What could possibly happen to her in this sleepy town? It was so weird because every time she allowed herself to acknowledge it, she felt a rush of jumbled emotions that were centred around this place and its people. They were good emotions, hope, a tinge of excitement mixed with anticipation, a sense of peace like she'd come home.

And that very inconvenient physical attraction she felt toward a certain policeman.

Dammit.

She picked up her bags and crossed the room where she switched off the lights before exiting the office taking care to engage the deadlock. The door clicked shut behind her. Head low, in an unconscious imitation of Miss Collins earlier, Tessa trudged down Main Street, heading for the Royal Hotel. If she was lucky, she might score a decent meal and a glass of white before the long, cold walk to her motel. What a fool she'd been to leave the rental car at the motel, thinking that a brisk walk in the morning would be beneficial to her health. She'd almost frozen solid! *I'll drive tomorrow.*

When she pushed through the swing doors into the front bar, a timber paneled room, warmth rushed to greet her. She could have dropped to her knees in thanks. Instead she hurried over to the open fireplace and held her numb gloved hands toward the flickering flames. Pins and needles heralded the return of blood flow to her fingers. The stinging in her face subsided and she hoped her nose no longer glowed red. She dabbed the tip with a tissue from her pocket, glad feeling had returned. Balling her hands and flexing her fingers, she sighed with relief and crossed to the bar where two wrinkled, weathered old men perched on their stools enjoying glasses of dark beer. One of them had a white cockatoo perched on his shoulder.

The bartender leaned his elbows on the bar and gave her an appreciative look up and down. A burly man in his fifties with red hair and a roguish twinkle in his eyes, he grinned and said, "What can I do you for Miss?"

"A small glass of house white, please. Oh and any chance of a meal?"

"Sure thing, sugar." He seemed to think they were in on a secret, because he winked before turning around and retrieving a wine bottle from a mini-bar fridge. After pouring her glass, he leaned on the bar like he had nowhere else to go and was settling in for a lengthy chat.

An encompassing glance around the room, told Tessa business was slow. Apart from the two pensioners fronting the bar and noisily gulping their beer the place was empty.

"Too cold out," said the barman as if in answer to her unspoken question.

"Tell me about it," Tessa muttered before taking a sip of her wine, wishing for a magic wand to make her car appear outside.

The guy flexed his pectorals and placed his forefinger against his nose. "This is nothin', sugar. Wait until winter really sets in."

Tessa shuddered. "How much?"

"I'll add it to your food bill." He jerked his head toward a door at the back of the room. "Through there and first door on your left, is the dining room. Gayle will look after you."

Picking up her glass, Tessa nodded and followed his directions.

Two hours later, she'd finished a surprisingly tasty dinner of lamb cutlets and three vegies and had just taken her last mouthful of piping, hot tea. The waitress bustled up and laid her bill on the table before taking away the empty tea pot. Palming her mobile, Tessa checked the time. Almost six-thirty. She smiled as she pressed the number for home.

It was answered on the third ring.

"Mummy!"

Tessa's heart clenched. "Sweetheart, how are you?"

"Good," sang Kaylee. "Guess what? I came second in a maths quiz today at school and Maki's made my favourite for dessert - fried ice-cream."

"That's great, Kaylee, well done. I'm proud of you." Trust Maki to ensure her baby's small success was celebrated. She owed him so much. Her fingers clutched the phone tighter. "How's that homework coming along?"

"Mum!" Kaylee dragged out the word.

"Try to get some more done tonight, okay hon? Now, Kaylee, remember I said I'd be home late tomorrow night? Well it looks like I need to stay here another day."

"Will you be home then for certain?"

Remembering how difficult it had been to pin the mayor down, Tessa hesitated before saying, "Sweetheart, I'll try."

"I guess that's okay."

"Have you had your bath?"

"After ice cream."

Tessa grinned. "Okay then, sweetheart. You run off and have your dessert. Giving you a big hug and kiss. Love you baby."

"Love you too, Mummy. Maki wants to say hi."

The sound of breathing and footsteps came over the phone. Tessa gained the distinct impression her old friend was taking the phone out of the room. Her pulse quickened.

"All okay there, *Chan*?" Maki said quietly.

"Yes, but I've been delayed. I'm so sorry, Maki, but I may need to be here an extra day." Sweat formed on her upper lip while she waited for his response. "What's happened?"

"Maybe nothing but I thought a man watched the house this morning. Again, this afternoon, same man."

Oh God. It hadn't been a ruse. He did know where she lived!

"Did you catch a good look at him?" she whispered. She could still be wrong, just her crazy imagination playing tricks.

"He stood in shadow of building. Too far away."

"What made you think he's the same man?"

"Same colour trousers. Cream and grey army trousers."

"Camouflage pattern." Tessa squeezed her eyes shut, her chest one huge thump of fear. "It's sports day tomorrow. Keep Kaylee home from school."

"I will do this, *Chan*. Do not worry, I will see her safe."

"I know you will, Maki. Thank you." But if the watcher was who she dreaded, then Tessa knew only too well what he was capable of. One elderly man with such a gentle nature as Maki would be no match for that bastard.

She spoke for a few more minutes doing her best to sound upbeat and in control while all the time, her life was splintering into fragments around her. When she hung up, she sat there in the empty dining room for a long time, her thoughts chasing themselves like manic mice trapped in a wheel.

Her mobile rang. Hand shaking she looked at the screen. Caller ID blocked. She switched it onto silent and dropped it back onto the table. Thirty seconds later it vibrated with another incoming call. Caller ID blocked.

Barely able to breathe, Tessa turned the phone off.

Despite the heat from the lit fireplace, she felt as cold as a long dead corpse. No closer to a solution, she dragged herself to her feet and left the warmth of the pub for the walk back to the motel.

Every step of the way, she shuddered and shook, her gaze darting first right then left, seeing the monster from her past in every shadow.

CHAPTER SEVEN

It was a noise that woke her. An alien noise and what sounded like the distant laughter of a child. Could it have been a kookaburra? If so, that was one weird bird. Tessa fought the fog of sleep and, yawning, cracked open her eyes a slit.

Cautiously, her gaze slid around her motel room. Nothing had changed from the night before - no surprises. Her small suitcase still remained upright, fully packed and zipped ready for instant flight, her boots neatly stacked next to her briefcase. Her handbag was sitting on the bedside table. Nothing out of place and very little sign that she inhabited the room. She'd always lived this way; a habit programmed into her when she was very young and when life with her mother was precarious.

Hee-haw. There it was again! A donkey...*a donkey!*

"Don't tell me. Don't tell me," Tessa muttered, scrambling out of bed and scattering doona and pillows left, right and centre. Her foot tangled in a blanket and down she went, landing hard on her hands and knees. "Ow!"

Wrestling with the knotted fabric, she finally freed herself and limped to the door. Hand poised over the deadbolt, she chewed her lip for a second. Caution and her curiosity came a tie. Slipping the lock she eased open the door a fraction and squinted through the crack.

Delight exploded in her heart and she flung the door wide.

"Kaylee!" Tessa rushed outside and swept her daughter up into her arms, swinging her around and around.

Kaylee, her face buried against Tessa's chest, giggled and shrieked and held her just as tight. At last, Tessa placed her daughter carefully on her feet, then cupping her cheeks looked down into her dear face.

"Surprise," Kaylee said, grinning widely and revealing a gap where her top left baby eye tooth had been.

Tessa kissed her and ran a hand lovingly over the top of her daughter's hair. Now that the initial delight had faded, fear took its place ransoming her breath.

"It's a lovely surprise but what..." she looked over Kaylee's head to where her friend, Makishi Fukuka a smile breaking over his walnut-wrinkled face, leaned against the bonnet of his

1973 Dodge ute. A familiar white and grey muzzle poked between the timber slats of a built-in box that stood another one and a half metres above the cabin roof. The donkey stretched its mouth wide as if grinning, showing large yellowing teeth and a pink tongue.

Maki shook his head quickly and, heart pounding, Tessa bit back her question. Instead saying, "Let's go inside shall we? I need to get dressed before I turn into an ice block. It's freezing out here."

Kaylee giggled and skipped toward the door.

Maki pushed off the car and said, "Today is weekend. Since you did not come home, we come to you for holiday."

"I'm sorry about that, Maki." Tessa pulled a face. "The mayor still hasn't given me the green light to send the proposal. Apparently, he's had a family emergency and hasn't had time to read it over." In fact, apart from constantly emailing or texting Donaldson, she'd loafed about doing very little. The time had hung heavily on her hands so she'd walked and explored the small town. But in doing so, she'd become more and more aware of how desperately the people here needed help.

She hadn't seen Dodge since he'd taken her for a tea break at his grandmother's house two days ago. She hadn't seen his gran either for that matter or any of her CWA cronies. It was as if they were deliberately avoiding her.

What if Dodge had told them about her past?

Rubbing her chilled hands together as they walked inside her motel room, she gloomily admitted she hated the idea they might well have turned against her. She left Kaylee chatting away with Maki while she showered and dressed in her blue jeans and her cream jumper. Having only packed the barest essentials, she was heartily sick of wearing the same clothes alternate days and handwashing them in the bathroom sink every night.

"How about breakfast?" Hopefully, Mrs McLean could offer something other than cornflakes and toast.

"A second breakfast." Kaylee giggled quoting from one of her favourite movies. "We had bananas and a milkshake at the takeaway shop."

"Bananas are good." Tessa grinned and led the way from her motel room along the outside of the building and into the main reception area where the dining room was situated.

Mrs McLean was manning the front desk when they entered and she smiled. "I see your daughter and friend found you okay, Miss Gibson."

"Please call me, Tessa. Yes, thank you. Are you open for breakfast?"

"Definitely." The other woman's eyes brightened. "We have eggs and bacon on the menu today."

"Sounds fabulous. We'll take three, all scrambled, please."

Her daughter chatted away all through their meal, giving Tessa a run down on school, her friends, how much she hated some boy in her class who kept pulling her hair and what she'd watched on television with Maki. *This is what I've missed.* Misty-eyed Tessa listened and re-affirmed her determination to keep her daughter safe and well. But first she had to find out what had happened to make Maki leave the city.

Mrs McLean entered when they'd finished eating to clear away the table.

"Mrs McLean, would you happen to have a carrot or an apple my daughter could give Tails. That's our donkey," Tessa explained.

"Certainly. I couldn't help hearing him this morning." The woman grimaced.

"Sorry about that and he's a she, a jenny donkey. We'll make alternate arrangements."

"If you could, I think that would be for the best. Our guests are usually over-nighter's, businessmen for the main part and they need their sleep."

Tessa nodded. She could well imagine the motel owner would be keen not to upset her regular customers although she suspected they were few and far between.

When the woman returned bearing both apples and carrots, Tessa asked, "Mrs Mclean, do you have any ideas where we could agist Tails? It would only be for a few days but we'd need a paddock with some kind of shelter for her."

"You could try Mrs Brown and Miss Collins. They have a fenced field behind their garden that has an old stable building. It might suit and I know they'd be grateful for the money. They wouldn't charge a great deal either." She gave directions to their house.

Tessa thanked her and they trooped out of the dining room. While Kaylee fed Tails, Tessa and Maki stood well back out of her daughter's hearing.

"Okay, Maki *Chan*. What happened?" Arms folded, Tessa turned to her friend. His face settled into anxious wrinkles.

Trepidation was a hard fist in the pit of her belly.

"Phone calls start morning after you say you are delayed. When I answer, no one speaks. I hear breathing. Yesterday, I bring Kaylee home from school. Your back door that opens onto fire escape is open. I locked it." His grim eyes met hers. "I search but nothing has been stolen."

"Oh my God," breathed Tessa, her heart pounding. She wiped her clammy palms over her thighs, hating the way they trembled. "What if he followed you?"

Maki tilted his head and smirked. "Impossible. We pack that night. I told Little Star we were going on a secret holiday. I check first but no one watches. We leave at three in the morning down the fire escape. I use a shopping trolley to push bags. Catch taxi one block away that takes us to the train station where we travel to Blackheath. Another taxi to the refuge. We load up Tails and luggage into my car and we come. Did I do right, *Chan*?"

Tessa squeezed his outstretched hand. "Yes. Thank you."

"Who is this man that watches? Is he the one you told me about?"

"Yes."

Maki nodded. "I understand."

"Looks like Tails has eaten all the food. How about we go for a walk and check out this field?"

They set off after Tessa insisted Kaylee pull the hood of her sheepskin jacket up over her head and zip up the jacket. The morning was crisp, the air fresh with a sharpness that caused Tessa's skin to tingle and the early morning fog was lifting allowing the straggling beams of sunlight to play and glisten over the frosty ground.

Walking was slow as Kaylee was forever darting off to hang over a fence to call to a mob of kangaroos, exclaim over a cow or chase after any bird that alighted onto the ground in front of them. But Tessa didn't mind. It was wonderful to have her daughter and Maki's company. Even though her mind was full of worry, she couldn't help enjoying the moment.

She led the way along Main Street after they'd spent a good twenty minutes walking about Lette Park. Maki remained quiet and thoughtful as they passed boarded up buildings and the shabby occupied ones.

"We'll walk down the river, perhaps after lunch once we have Tails settled somewhere," Tessa said.

"These people are in need," stated Maki, his tone disapproving.

"I know and I hate myself for what I'm doing." Tessa clenched her jaw and looked away. "Here we are. Let's hope the old ladies are home."

She mounted the two steps onto the front porch, noting with dismay the number of missing floorboards and knocked.

From somewhere inside a strident voice demanded, "Who is it?"

"It's me, Mrs Brown. Tessa Gibson," she yelled.

A few seconds later came the thump of footsteps along the hall and the door opened to reveal Pamela Brown, grey eyebrows raised. "Goodness. It is you. And who do you have here?"

"This is my daughter, Kaylee and Makishi Fukuka."

"Who is it, Pam?" called Miss Collins.

"It's that government girl and she's got a daughter," Mrs Brown bellowed down the hall.

"Who?"

"Tessa Gibson!"

"Oh, dear me. What a lovely surprise." Miss Collins popped out of the shadowy recesses of the hallway peering down toward where her sister blocked the door. "Let them in, Pam. I'll put the kettle on."

"She's got a Jap with her." Mrs Brown practically vibrated with outrage where she stood. Her nose quivered and her glare would have been capable of stopping a Mack truck. "I'll not have any Japanese in my house."

Tessa glared back. "Maki happens to be a personal friend of mine and you are downright insulting."

"Our father fought those scoundrels in the war."

"And that was a bloody long time ago. Get over it." Tessa flung her head up and stared the older woman down.

Suddenly, the gentle Miss Collins pushed past her sister and beamed. "Don't worry about Pam. She was devoted to our father. I've got the tea made, so come inside. We don't get many visitors. I hope you'll excuse the state of our home."

Tessa smiled. "Thank you but we'll stay out here. I've come…"

"Heavens to Betsy," snapped Mrs Brown stepping aside and waving them forward like a traffic controller. "Get inside. That child is looking a bit peeky."

"What?" Tessa spun around to see Kaylee leaning against Maki. Her eyes had drifted half-closed. Guilt was a hot sword thrust through her heart. She never should have allowed her to walk so far.

"Come in. Come in. A hot cuppa and a scone will fix her up." Mrs Brown grabbed Tessa's arm with surprising strength and pulled her over the threshold. "You better come in too," she sniffed, obviously referring to Maki.

She led the way down the hall to the kitchen at the rear of the house and where an old fuel stove warmed the room. It was sparsely furnished with a laminate table in the centre and two timber chairs. Faded gingham curtains framed the only window, which looked out over well-tended garden beds. Maki immediately made his way to the window and stood stiffly while he stared at the view.

Hating the thought she may be eating what could be the last of their food, Tessa refused everything but the hot cuppa although she allowed Kaylee to sit at the table and eat the offered hot-buttered scone and jam. Instead, she joined Maki near the window in a show of comradeship and sipped tea out of a bone-china cup that looked to be almost as old as the two sisters.

She told them they needed agistment for a donkey for a few days and upon hearing the stables had a water-tight roof sealed the deal. Eager to escape Mrs Brown's hostility and the curiosity she could see sparkling in both ladies eyes, Tessa gulped down her tea. Colour had returned to her daughter's pale cheeks and Tessa murmured something about 'getting on'.

Catching Kaylee's hand in hers, she thanked the ladies and headed to the front door. Upon opening it, she gasped.

Poised in the doorway, and craning her neck to look past Tessa, was Edwina Lette. Behind her, was Dodge an inscrutable expression on his face as his gaze fell on the little girl at Tessa's side.

"I knew it was you," Dodge's grandmother announced in a satisfied voice. "Spotted you from the upstairs verandah. Amazing what you can see from up there. What are you doing here?"

Save me now from nosy old ladies. But no fairy godmother appeared with a wand to whisk Tessa away. Through gritted teeth, she said, "Minding my own business."

"Now, now, don't get miffy. You're as bad as Dodge."

Heat bloomed on Tessa's face. The old woman was right, she'd been downright rude. But she wasn't used to having her every movement commented upon or being on the receiving end of advice – however well meant. From under her lashes, Tessa peeked at Dodge. There was a twinkle in his hazel eyes that warmed her through and through. Made her feel like he understood how she felt. Maybe he wasn't that inscrutable after all. He winked. Maybe he hadn't been avoiding her. He could have been busy.

"Edwina," boomed Mrs Brown hovering behind Tessa's small family. "The girl needs a place for her donkey. And she has a child. And she has a Jap for a friend. Look!"

Everyone looked.

First at Kaylee staring wide-eyed at the adults and then onto Maki behind her.

A flush bloomed high on Maki's cheekbones and he shuffled his feet.

"A donkey! Well, I never. You are full of surprises." Edwina Lette grinned like she'd been given the winning Lotto numbers.

No mention of her daughter, Tessa noted. No mention of her having an elderly Japanese man for a friend.

"How's the grant coming along?" Edwina pressed.

"The mayor is proving hard to catch. I can't send it off until he's signed the form." Even Tessa could hear the frustration in her voice.

"Typical." Edwina snorted. "Looks like you'll be staying here a while longer."

"I guess." Tessa recalled what or who could well be waiting for her when she returned home and her blood froze in her veins. She shivered.

Eyes sharp, like she could read every thought inside Tessa's head, Dodge's grandmother said, "One thing is for certain, you can't stay in that mouldy motel with your little girl. A child needs space to run and play. You can stay with us."

"What?" Tessa gaped, restraining herself with the greatest of difficulty from at looking at Dodge to ascertain his reaction to the invitation.

Edwina snapped her fingers. Bending down so she was on level with Kaylee, she smiled, her voice softening as she said, "You can meet our ghost."

Kaylee squealed, "A ghost?"

"Yep. Her name is Matilda."

"My name is Kaylee." She held out her hand and the old lady took it and shook with no trace of a smile on her face.

"I'm Edwina Lette and this is my grandson, Dodge. You can call me Gran, too. Just like Dodge here."

"Dodge. That's weird." Kaylee frowned as she stared at him.

He said easily, "I'm good at running with the ball when I play footy."

Satisfied with his explanation, Kaylee smiled shyly and shook his extended hand. Dodge then offered it to Maki who stepped past Tessa out onto the porch. There, both men eyed each other, taking each other's measure before shaking.

"Makishi Fukuka." Maki then bowed.

Dodge dipped his chin in response.

His gran rubbed her hands. "Now that's out of the way, how about we get your gear and get you settled in?"

"I really think its best we stay in the motel," Tessa said.

"Rubbish." Edwina took Kaylee's hand and together they stepped off the porch. "Come over for dinner tonight, Pam and Beatrix. We're having lamb roast."

"Very well, Edwina. We'll bring some stewed rhubarb," said Mrs Brown, before closing the front door on them and cutting off any idea Tessa may have had of retreating in that direction.

"Mummy!" Voice high with excitement, Kaylee looked over her shoulder at her mother. "They have a ghost."

"There is no such thing as ghosts." Tessa marched off after them and found Dodge falling into step beside her. Kaylee appeared to have regained her strength from the way she was skipping beside the old lady and if her giggling was anything to go by.

"Don't mind my friend, Pam, Tessa," called Edwina over her shoulder. "She's always abrupt with people she likes. Poor thing has never really gotten over losing her husband and son in the floods of 1955."

Tessa immediately felt guilty she'd harboured resentment over the old woman's abrasive manner. Coming so close, twice, to losing her daughter she could fully understand the lady's anguish. Next time they spoke, she'd make an effort to be nicer.

"We can't possibly stay with you," Tessa said now to Dodge, thinking about how this probably wasn't the brightest idea, given he was a representative of the law. And then there was the temptation he represented as a man.

"I don't see why not. There's plenty of room although I have to warn you, most of the house hasn't been renovated yet. I'll lock those rooms where the flooring is a bit shonky."

"We still can't stay here." *Live under the same roof as you and pretend I don't feel anything? No. That's just too hard.*

"Gran will be glad of the company. Look at those two. They look like soul mates." He

gestured at the couple prancing ahead.

"I know and that's what worries me." Tessa couldn't deny that was another concern. She could feel a headache coming on.

Dodge laughed. "Gran is a bit eccentric but she'll look after your little girl."

Maki, who until now had been ambling along behind, caught Tessa's hand and tugged. She leaned closer while he murmured in her ear, "This may be good idea, *Chan*. Think, you will be off radar. No name in motel registry."

Tessa sucked in her breath. He was right. Her thoughts raced. Staying at Fig Tree Lodge would be a good place to hide and lie low. No way to trace her, especially if she continued to use cash to pay her expenses. If they stayed there until the funds from the government came through, they could disappear to the north leaving no trail and where they'd assume new names.

New identities.

The perfect plan to keep her daughter safe.

Decision made, Tessa looked over to where Dodge waited, watching her and wearing his cop-face. Until then, she hadn't noticed they'd actually stopped walking. He wore his beanie pulled low over his forehead. A few curls poked out above his eyes. They looked soft and oh so beguiling. *Be strong. Focus.*

Taking a deep breath, she said, "We accept your invitation. But we'll pay our way."

His slow smile sent a flash of raw heat scalding her body. Shoving his hands deep in his jacket pockets, he drawled, "Don't worry. I know exactly what I want from you."

CHAPTER EIGHT

In silence, Dodge, Tessa and Maki crossed the road and passed through the gate of Fig Tree Lodge. Looking up at the grand, old house, Dodge experienced the familiar sweet, sharp sense of homecoming that never failed to assail him. It didn't matter if he'd been gone for hours or years. The feeling was always the same. Fig Tree Lodge was rooted in his past and offered the promise of his future.

He looked over to see Tessa's daughter and his gran standing under the old fig tree and smiled. Awe was clearly etched on the little girl's face as she gazed into the maze of towering branches. Gran must have been telling her about a bird of some description because she had crouched lower, her head close to the little girl and Gran had her arm raised, pointing upwards.

There was something about the picture they made, like they'd always stood there, as if they both belonged.

Tessa walked beside him down the drive and he heard her quick, indrawn breath and wondered whether she'd had the same thought.

From around the side of the house, Rufus appeared, barking, tail wagging furiously as he raced over to Gran and Kaylee. He skidded to a halt and rolled over onto his back, legs in the air. Laughing, Kaylee dropped to her knees and rubbed his belly.

He had a sudden vision of the young girl playing on a tyre swing and made an instant mental note to organise that pronto. Maybe he'd build a tree house for her. He could well imagine her delight, she appeared to be a good kid, easily pleased and appreciative of anything someone did for her. So very like her mother. Except her mother had a reserve that was hard to break through and made climbing Mount Everest appear an easy feat. But then, he had been interrogating her. And that was bound to put anyone's back up. Even more so, when they had something to hide.

His gaze slid past Tessa who was smiling at her daughter and lingered for a moment on the old Japanese guy who was examining a clump of daffodils growing beside the drive. For the life of him, he couldn't work out how this bloke figured in Tessa's life. But one thing was as plain as the nose on his face, Mr Fukuka was treated with affection and trust by both Tessa and her daughter.

He couldn't be a relative. So who was he? Gran was right. Tessa had secrets and he needed to dig them out quick smart. There was too much at stake here for both the town and his family. Dodge hadn't missed the fear etched on Tessa's face when he'd appeared in Lansky's office the other day. She'd gone so white he'd wondered for a second whether she'd fall to the ground. She was afraid of something or someone. And he intended to find out exactly what she was hiding. Having her under his roof, gave him the ideal opportunity to learn more about her. All he had to do was keep his hands to himself. That wasn't going to be easy. Not when all he wanted to do was wrap her in his arms and protect her.

Thinking of secrets made him remember the donkey.

Dodge grinned as they stepped onto the verandah. That was one secret he'd never have guessed. With a feeling like resignation he realised he wouldn't rest until he knew everything there was to know about Tessa. "I'll show you around and we'll allocate some rooms for you. Okay for you and Kaylee to kip together?"

"That's fine." Tessa smiled.

Gosh, she's gorgeous. Without stopping to think, Dodge brushed his fingertip over her petal-soft cheek, feeling her quiver under his touch. His blood heating to ignition point, he stepped closer drinking in the rich, Greek-coffee depths of her dewy eyes, longing to feel the imprint of her body against his. He'd spent quite a few hours fantasising over doing just that and more, ever since he'd first laid eyes on her. Keeping his hands to himself was not going to be as easy as he'd imagined, he admitted wryly.

The sound of the old Japanese guy giving a gentle cough brought Dodge to his senses. *I can't believe I just did that in front of everyone.*

Face hot, he spun around and opened the door wide for Tessa to enter. She rushed inside apparently eager to put some distance between them. Her Japanese friend followed, a heavy frown on his face. Then his Gran was there with Kaylee at her side. Gran nudged him with her elbow and winked.

Rolling his eyes, he toed off his boots. He would have given his left lung for his grandmother to have missed that weak moment. Now, she'd swing into matchmaking mode and heaven help him and Tessa.

Nothing on this Earth could stop Gran once she was on a mission.

The tour of the house took close to an hour. Not that it was that big, but in every room Gran insisted on stopping and giving a long spiel about who'd built what, owned what, slept there, ate there and on and on.

Having heard it all before, Dodge was yawning by the time they'd returned to the front foyer. Tessa looked dazed, her friend thoughtful and Kaylee visibly drooping as she sagged against her mother. Tessa wrapped her arm around her daughter and hugged her close, frowning while she soothed her other hand over the girl's hair.

Her actions made Dodge wonder whether the kid had something wrong with her. She did appear to be unusually pale. Although tall for her age, she seemed thin with fragile-looking wrists. There was no denying she was her mother's daughter. They shared the same dark brown eyes and lashes and both had thick, long hair. But whereas Tessa's was straight, dark and shot with red, Kaylee had long curls and was a lighter brown with blonde streaks.

"Lunchtime I think," Gran said, her gaze fixed on the little girl. She hadn't missed the kid's lack of energy.

Tessa looked over at Makishi. "We need to sort Tails out. The donkey," she added when Dodge raised his eyebrows.

"I'll drive you back to the motel after lunch. Kaylee can stay here with Gran," he said, smiling.

"Yes, Kaylee can keep me company while I take my usual afternoon nap on the lounge. I think we've got two or three Trixie Beldon books she may like to read."

As far as he was aware, Gran had never rested during the day in her life!

Tessa glanced between them. "Thank you," she said quietly and Dodge knew she was thanking them for more than lunch.

As soon as the meal was over, it took a matter of minutes to tidy everything away with Tessa and Maki assisting. Gran and the little girl curled up on the lounge together in the main drawing room with a book in their hands and Rufus snug in his bed in front of the fire. Tessa gave her daughter a kiss before they left the house in his Landrover.

The drive to the motel was short and silent.

The Japanese guy stared out the window and Tessa who'd insisted on sitting in the back appeared to be lost in her thoughts, judging by the faint frown she wore.

Dodge wished she'd share them with him. The need to solve her problems and bring a smile to her face grew stronger with every passing hour. His fingers tapped the steering wheel, as he turned the car off the road into the motel carpark. Tessa opened her door and hopped out, before he'd turned off the engine.

I'm a sucker where complicated women are concerned. From all the partners he could have teamed up with out of training, he'd gravitated to

Sara. And look what kind of mess that had ended up being. His one long-term relationship, he'd hooked up with a girl called Izzy who'd just come out of an abusive marriage. As soon as she was emotionally strong enough, she'd disappeared into the sunset – literally, heading off on a one way ticket to Europe.

Which left Tessa.

A girl with fear in her heart and shadows in her eyes, what looked like a sickly child and an unlikely friendship with a man old enough to be her grandfather.

Complicated wasn't the word.

***

Tessa checked the tiny ensuite one last time. All clear. No trace of her occupancy could be found either in here or in the motel room. *Perfect.* She hurried outside and found Dodge had already loaded her bag and briefcase into his Landrover.

When she peered into the back, she found Dodge and Maki had already transferred the luggage Maki had brought with him.

"I will see to Tails," Maki said climbing behind the wheel of his ute and shutting the door. Tessa knew he was concerned his pet had been cooped up for such an unfamiliar length of time and he'd be eager to ensure she was settled before he left her alone.

"See you back at the Lodge," she said waving him on the way. To Dodge, she added, "I'll settle up with Mrs McLean. There's no need to wait for me. I can find my way easily to your house."

Without waiting for Dodge's response, Tessa hurried off to the reception area where Mrs McLean handed over the bill.

Smiling pleasantly, Tessa said, "This isn't correct, Mrs McLean. You haven't charged me for the extra week I booked two days ago."

"I can't bill you for what you didn't use, dear."

Tessa hesitated, remembering the run-down condition of her room. It was plain as the nose on her face, the McLeans were short on funds and she couldn't see much business coming their way. What would it matter if she helped them out a little? It wouldn't be long and she'd have more money than she'd ever dreamed of.

"No, I insist." She performed a quick calculation of her bank balance and the cash remaining in her wallet. "I'm sure you would have turned away someone else to keep my room available. I'll pay for the end of the week."

"Well, if you're certain..." Mrs McLean's voice trailed off. She did up another invoice and Tessa handed over the money. "Thank you, dear."

Leaving the woman smiling down at the bills in her hand, Tessa turned around and made for the door.

Dodge leaned against the wall. He straightened and mouthed, 'well done' and the hot rush of pleasure at his approval flustered her. Her heart twisted. *What will he think of me, when he learns the truth?*

His hand curled around hers, the warmth and smoothness of his palm was reassuring. Together they walked to the carpark.

"That was a good thing you did back there."

She shivered at the deep timbre of his voice. "This is a business trip. I can claim expenses," she lied. The words tasted bitter in her mouth.

"Mmm."

Her heart skipped a beat. Was he onto her? Or did he suspect her of ulterior motives? Deciding retreat was the best option, she slipped her hand out of his and hurried to her rental car.

The remainder of the day, Tessa and Kaylee spent settling into Fig Tree Lodge. Not that it took that long to unpack a few items into the massive Edwardian timber wardrobe and matching dresser.

But Tessa had decided a long walk along the riverbank might be pushing her daughter's endurance, so spending the afternoon ambling about the gardens was the next best thing. There certainly were sufficient items of interest here to capture Kaylee's attention. Already she was full of plans of picking the ripe vegetables and plucking the fruit from the lower branches of the orange, mandarin and lime trees. She'd been fascinated with the chickens in their pen and their amazing hen house and would have spent all day in there if she could.

"We're not staying for too long," she warned Kaylee later that afternoon as she sat on the double four-poster bed, her daughter curled against her while Tessa brushed her hair.

"Why not? I like it here." Kaylee turned around revealing a mutinous pout.

I like it too, but I'm never going to say it out loud. From under her lashes she sent an appreciative glance around the bedroom. The room could have been made for her.

The walls were painted crimson above the picture railing with the lower section having a glorious velvet embossed wallpaper. The corner bedroom had two French doors that opened out onto the upper verandah. Heavy crimson drapes hung over both and also the one window to keep out any draughts. A floral patterned armchair picked out in emerald green and a lighter pink was strategically positioned beside the fireplace and with a small circular table positioned next to it. Over the floorboards lay a massive Turkish rug. There were quite a few of the boards a lighter colour than the others, suggesting they'd been replaced, probably from rot. Tessa looked up at the ceiling to the intricately carved plaster. Squinting, she could just make out where the plaster had been repaired, no doubt a leaking roof was the culprit.

Tessa set her jaw. "This isn't our home. Soon we'll be moving on." No need to go into exactly where they were going. Not yet. The fewer people who knew her plans, the better. Kaylee was such an open child, she wouldn't dream of holding her tongue and not chatting about their lives.

"I don't want to go back to Sydney."

If I have my way, we'll never go back. "Let's not talk about this now. What do you think of this bed?"

"It's a princess bed," squealed Kaylee.

"And you're the princess." Tessa hugged her.

Kaylee giggled. "I hope there won't be any peas under the mattress."

"Let's hope not." Tessa laughed. "I've finished, no more knots. How about a French braid?"

Kaylee nodded. "Then it's your turn, Mummy."

"Deal."

"You have to wear your red dress tonight, Mummy. It's like a celebration."

"I was going to wear jeans."

"No way." Kaylee planted her hands on her narrow hips. "Besides, I want to wear the medieval dress you made me for the school play last year. I want you to dress up with me. I made sure Maki packed both dresses. I couldn't leave them behind. " She added in a whisper, "I never got to wear it."

No, you were in hospital at the time. Tessa's throat tightened. "You've grown a bit taller since then but I think it should fit as I made it so it trailed on the ground."

"Hurry up, Mummy. I don't want to miss anything."

Fifteen minutes later they were both ready. Tessa gave her reflection one final look before glancing down at her stockinged feet. It seemed kind of rude to wear shoes inside the house. She hadn't failed to notice how both Dodge and his grandmother left whatever footwear they'd worn outside, at the front door. In fact the last time she came inside the house, she'd tripped over Edwina's gumboots. And now she came to think about it, high heels could well mark the dining room's polished floorboards. Shrugging, she decided to forget about footwear.

Smiling, she held out her hand to her daughter and giggling, Kaylee clasped it. Together they walked down the wide hallway to the main staircase. Thankfully, both appeared to have been repaired.

Dodge had already warned them not to go out onto the upper balcony. Tessa would have preferred he'd locked the French doors but unfortunately he told her the keys to the old doors had been lost about twenty years ago.

They descended the stairs carefully with Kaylee holding her long skirt high so she didn't trip. When they entered the dining room, the place appeared full of people. The two sisters were present as was Mrs Miller who stood beside a tall, thin elderly man chatting with Maki. Tessa's gaze sought and found Dodge holding a glass of wine and deep in conversation with Lou dressed in maternity overalls with a fleecy pale blue jumper beneath.

Dodge looked up and met Tessa's eyes. The corners of his mouth edged into a smile as his gaze slid over her body then back to her face. Her tummy turned to mush at the sight of his broad shoulders clad in a knitted, long sleeve black shirt that clung to every hard-packed muscle he possessed. And he had quite a few.

Beneath her calf-length woollen dress, her knees trembled as her gaze travelled down him. Blue jeans emphasized the slimness of his hips and the lean length of his legs. He wore socks and Tessa was glad she'd decided against any shoes.

"My, don't you too look fine," Edwina Lette said. "Now, let's take a good look at you. Turn around."

There was a general murmur of approval. Tessa gave a strained smile while Kaylee dropped her mother's hand and obediently gave a twirl.

"Such a lovely dress. She looks exactly like a princess," Mrs Miller said.

"Mummy made it for me."

"Mummy is very clever," drawled Dodge. The quiet timbre of his voices sent goosebumps prickling Tessa's skin. He crossed the room to draw her arm through his and lead her over to the few faces she hadn't recognized. "Jonas Miller is our rector."

The rector gave a vague smile without ceasing his monologue on the difficulties he was experiencing in repairing stained glass windows.

"Doctor Warner."

The doctor, an elderly gentleman with wire-rimmed glasses perched on the tip of his bulbous nose, squeezed her hand.

"Mrs Esther Ainslie, a retired librarian who very kindly runs our small library for one day a week."

"Lou, how's the food coming along?" called Ms Lette.

Louise checked her watch. "Ooops! Should be ready. Dodge give us a hand, wont you."

Her comment was more of a demand than a question and Tessa couldn't help notice how quickly he responded. Was it because he was used to taking orders from her, seeing how she was his sergeant? Or something else?

In the sudden movement toward the dining table, Maki appeared at her side.

"Is Tails okay?" she asked.

Maki smiled. "I checked half an hour ago. She is eating and have shut her into the stable for the night."

"That's good."

"Pretty dress. The policeman was impressed." Frowning, he looked in the direction of the kitchen and Tessa laughed to cover her flush of delight.

"Do you think so?" The words were out before she could stop herself.

Maki turned back to her and searched her face. "He is an honest man."

Her brief moment withered leaving nothing but the coldness of dead ashes in her heart. "I know."

They shared a glance of mutual understanding. There was no need for either to say any more. Both knew an honest cop would never turn a blind eye if he ever found out what Tessa intended to do.

At that moment, Dodge entered bearing a heavy silver platter from which came the succulent, mouth-watering aroma of roast lamb and rosemary. His glinting gaze seemed to look first for her. His slow smile was brilliant with anticipation and promise.

Drawing a deep breath, Tessa turned away.

I can't afford to get involved. She pulled out a chair as far away from his as possible and when she glanced up, his smile had vanished.

CHAPTER NINE

On Sunday, Tessa took Kaylee for a walk along the riverbank where they spent some time watching the ducks and waterfowl. In the afternoon, she made Kaylee do maths exercises and practice her spelling in their bedroom, doing her best to limit their contact with Dodge and his grandmother. The last thing she wanted was for Kaylee to become too fond of these people. She closed her mind to the little voice that whispered she was really protecting herself.

Throughout the day, she kept texting and emailing the mayor but it wasn't until Monday morning around nine thirty before he responded and gave her the go ahead to lodge the grant. He apologised for his slow response and mentioned how he'd had to drive his elderly mother-in-law to Moree Hospital after she'd fallen.

Another reminder of the state of the town's facilities. Or lack thereof.

This is not my problem, she reminded herself.

Dodge had left early for work and Maki had disappeared after muttering about seeing to Tails. She thought about the amount of typing she had left to do before she could send the proposal off seeing how the mayor had requested so many changes. Having a bored Kaylee with her at the solicitor's office would not be a good idea.

The sooner it's lodged, the quicker the money will be received. And that meant the faster they could leave town. Mobile in hand she finally tracked Edwina down in the partly renovated drawing room.

"Geez!" Tessa tossed her phone onto a lounge chair and raced across the room to brace her hands on the ladder. Staring up at the old lady perched on the uppermost rung while she scraped at the tattered remains of old wallpaper, she said, "You shouldn't be doing this, it isn't safe."

"Pwush. I'm used to it. Anyway there isn't anyone else." Edwina rubbed hard at the wall. The tools hanging from the carpenter's belt looped about her waist, jingled and jangled.

Tiny pieces of paper rained down into Tessa's upturned face. Blinking and blowing, she managed to shake the wallpaper remnants off.

"Where's that girl of yours?"

"She's in the garden, throwing a ball to Rufus."

"He'd love that. He's good with kids. So's Dodge for that matter. That's what this town needs, more children." Her voice was ripe with innuendo.

Scrape, scrape, scrape.

Wicked old woman. Knowing the old lady couldn't see her, Tessa allowed herself to grin. "About the rent I owe, I was thinking one hundred and twenty dollars should cover our room and board. The mayor has finally contacted me. If I can work all day uninterrupted, the final proposal could be sent off tonight. We'll leave the next morning."

But where will we go? I can't risk going back to my flat. Maybe another town like Bindarra Creek. One with a caravan park where we could get cheap accommodation and Maki could find agistment for Tails.

"What? Leave?" Edwina stopped attacking the wallpaper and glared down at Tessa. She shook her finger. "Your family only just arrived."

"This isn't a holiday," Tessa said firmly.

Edwina snorted. "Well it should be. The pair of you, both as pasty as sour milk. A few days in the country is what you need. You could stop stressing and relax and that girl of yours can do what girls of her age should be doing, playing and running about in the fresh air."

Tears clutched at her throat and Tessa had to swallow before she could speak. "That's very kind of you but it's out of the question. Kaylee has school and I need to work."

Edwina leaned back against the wall and spread her arms wide. The ladder wobbled. Tessa shifted her weight and held tight. Apparently oblivious, the old woman continued in a confiding tone, "Your generation takes life too seriously. Why in my day, we knew how to live..."

A sly smile spread over her face while her eyes twinkled mischievously.

Tessa could only imagine the kind of trouble this old woman would have gotten into – she would have embraced her life and to hell with the consequences. Dodge was lucky to have someone like her as his gran. Tessa hoped he appreciated her.

"Step back while I come down so we can discuss this properly, girl." Edwina Lette rammed her scraper into her pocket and clambered down the ladder to arrive at the bottom with no sign of breathlessness.

Gosh she's fit for her age. Then Tessa cringed when Edwina roared with laughter. She'd said it out loud.

"'Cause I am, that's the beauty of living out here. Always heaps to do. Now, let's have a cuppa and discuss this like rational people." Edwina took Tessa's elbow and steered her out of the room along the hall and into the kitchen.

"Ms Lette..." began Tessa, as she switched on the jug.

"Edwina will do." The old lady bustled about handing out mugs and spooning tea into the pot. "Cut us some fruit cake, there's a good girl. And while you're about it, give Kaylee a shout to come inside. She needs feeding."

Biting her tongue, Tessa stomped over to the screen door where she called for her daughter. She had cut the cake and laid the table with plates and the milk jug by the time Kaylee arrived out of breath and beaming, an equally panting dog at her side. Kaylee's cheeks were pink with colour and when she spotted the table she exclaimed, "Cake. Awesome."

"Drink your milk," Tessa said, pouring a big glass and pushing it across the table.

Kaylee pulled out a chair and tucked in.

Smiling, Tessa watched her daughter break off a piece of cake and hand it to the dog under the table. About to admonish her, Edwina nudged her.

"Leave her be."

Footsteps crunched on the gravel around the side of the house. *Dammit. I'd hoped for a quiet word with Edwina so we could leave without any fuss. That doesn't look like it's going to happen. Oh well. I have to make my position clear and there's no time like the present.*

The door swung open and Dodge strolled in, taking off his jacket and beanie at the same time.

"Great. I'm just in time for elevenses," he said placing his jacket on the hook.

Immediately the atmosphere in the kitchen changed, it seemed charged with the energy of his presence. His gaze swept over Tessa where she stood dithering beside the table, spoons in her hand. She couldn't seem to tear her eyes from him. His uniform gave him an aura of power and coupled with his inherent sex appeal, a girl would have to be dead not to notice.

"Do you like Lord of the Rings, too?" Kaylee stared at him wide eyed above the rim of her glass.

"Yep. Watched it five times already."

"Me too." A look that suggested adoration settled on her face.

"We can watch it tonight if you want to." Dodge winked at her as he sat and gave the dog a long scratch behind his ear. Rufus thumped his tail madly.

"Mummy?" squealed Kaylee.

"Kaylee, don't talk with your mouth full. And your homework has to be done before anything else." *What is he doing here? Checking up on us?* She tapped her toe against the floorboards. "Do you come home from work every day for morning tea?"

He leaned back in his chair, his gaze travelling from her hot face down her neck, seemed to linger an awfully long time in her chest region before wandering down her legs and back up again.

Her nipples tightened. She prayed he couldn't tell through the thickness of her jumper.

He grinned. "Only when there's something tasty on the menu."

He could tell.

Tessa could have thrown the tea towel at him.

With a dramatic sigh, his grandmother lowered herself into the chair.

A frown chased away Dodge's smirk. "Something wrong Gran?"

Eyes half-closed, Edwina fanned herself with a napkin. "I must have done too much this morning. I don't feel so good."

Tessa narrowed her eyes. There'd been no problem with her when she was racing up and down that ladder.

"Renovating a house this size is really a young person's job. My old bones..." she let her voice trail off suggestively.

Cunning old fox. Tessa ate cake and waited.

Dodge frowned. "Leave it. I'll get to it eventually."

"I know you will. You're such a good boy. But we can hardly advertise as a B&B if this place is falling down around our ears now can we?"

"It's not that bad." Dodge glanced around the kitchen.

"If I had some help," continued Edwina in a shaky voice. "Someone younger. Someone looking for a kind of working holiday while she waits for her next job."

Now we have it. Impassive, Tessa sipped her hot tea and fielded Dodge's eyes as he examined her face.

Obviously on a roll, Edwina added, "Tessa says they're leaving tomorrow."

"Bloody hell!" Dodge glared across the table.

"No! I don't want to go," wailed Kaylee pushing her half-empty glass roughly. It fell. Milk pooled. "I want to stay here with Gran and Dodge."

Calmly, Tessa placed her cup on the table and met Edwina's crafty gaze. *This is all your handiwork.* She rose to her feet and walked over to the sink for the sponge, saying, "The proposal will be finished tonight. I see no reason to stay any longer."

Kaylee began to cry. Teeth gritted, Tessa marched back to the table.

His frown positively ferocious, Dodge said, "It was also suggested that you stay to oversee the administering of the funds. At a fee of course." His mouth thinned.

Tessa shook inside. *I need more than a fee.* She looked at her daughter now crying into her hands and frustration rose. *All I want to do is protect her.* She said, "Nothing was decided. If you'll excuse me, I have work to do. Kaylee, gather some school books and come with me."

Kaylee stopped crying and shouted, "No."

"Kaylee, that's no way to speak to your mother."

Shaking, Tessa rounded on Dodge's grandmother. "This argument is your fault. We're leaving in the morning regardless of any meddling on your part."

Edwina fell back against her chair, eyes closed. "I don't feel well."

Chewing her lip, Tessa looked her over carefully. Her cheeks were pallid. There was sweat forming on her forehead. OMG, she really was sick. Tessa dropped the sponge and ran around the table to the old lady's side.

Dodge said, "She needs her pills." Shoving to his feet, he ran from the room.

While he was gone, Tessa dampened a tea towel and dabbed Edwina's face. Her hands trembled when she noted the bluish tinge to her lips and felt mean for yelling at the old girl.

Dodge returned, grabbed a glass of water and rushed to his gran's side. "Here you go. Swallow, Gran, and take a sip of water." He held the glass steady against her mouth.

Tessa stepped back and waited, her heart pounding, dread and self-loathing churning deep in her belly. She'd done this, caused this kind, if manipulative, old lady to have some type of attack. Kaylee flung herself at Tessa and wrapped her thin arms around her waist.

Feeling like bawling her eyes out herself, Tessa worried her bottom lip until finally Edwina opened her eyes. She looked tired and old.

Dodge asked, "Any better, Gran?" There was fear hidden in those quiet words.

Something hard and hot swelled painfully inside Tessa's chest when his grandmother said in a voice close to her usual manner, "'Cause I am, no need to fret, boy."

"I'll clear the table." Anxious to fix things, Tessa went to the sink, Kaylee clinging to her legs. She took a moment to crouch down and whisper, "It's okay, sweetheart."

"We were shouting, Mummy." Her mouth trembled. Another fat tear slipped down her cheeks.

"I know."

Then Dodge was there kneeling on the ground, his face serious as he said, "Gran has these turns now and again. She's got something wrong with her heart. Now she's had her tablet she'll be okay."

Kaylee looked up at Tessa. "Just like me, Mummy."

Silence fell in the room.

Tessa could feel Dodge and his grandmother staring at her. She forced herself to speak, "Yes. The sponge is on the table. Why don't you clean up that mess you made?"

Glad to help, Kaylee raced back to the table.

Dodge rose to his feet putting his hand out and catching hold of Tessa when she went to move past him. "Wait. What was that all about?"

"Which part?" She shrugged helplessly.

"All of it I guess. Kaylee?"

There was such kindness and concern in his eyes, Tessa said helplessly, "She was born with a type of congenital heart disease. When she was about eighteen months old, she had an operation that was supposed to fix the problem. Last year, she had to have another."

Nostrils flaring, Dodge sucked in a deep, shaky breath. "Bloody hell." He raised her hand to his mouth and kissed her knuckles. Looking at her, he whispered, "That must have been tough for both of you. I'm so sorry."

"The specialists think it was successful this time, but she has to take it easy. Plus, she's on medication for a while."

"Poor kid. I guess that's why she tires so quickly."

Tessa nodded and tugged her hand out of his.

"Mind if I tell Gran?" He glanced over to where his grandmother was hugging Kaylee.

"Sure. I guess." Tessa gave a brief smile.

A thoughtful frown wrinkling his forehead, Dodge dragged a hand through his hair. "Look, I know my grandmother can be a handful at times but she means well. You said yourself we could have the money in a matter of weeks. Why not stay? Gran could do with the company while I'm at work. If you're here, I know she won't be doing anything she shouldn't be doing. Plus, your daughter likes it here. It'll be good for her. Especially seeing how those two get on like a house on fire."

Tessa stared across the room.

Kaylee was busily smearing milk everywhere and talking nineteen to the dozen to Edwina who was nodding and eating cake. Apparently returned to her usual vigour, Edwina caught Tessa's eyes and winked.

"You really think I can stop your grandmother from doing anything she wants to do?"

Dodge laughed. "Probably not but having someone here with her would be a load off my mind."

"Your friend Lou must be due to start maternity leave any day now. She could do it. She lives here too anyway."

"I'm not certain what Lou has planned for the birth. She may decide to move closer to Armidale hospital or even Moree. Or Brisbane for that matter where her parents live. I don't want her to feel she's obligated to put her personal life on hold."

"But it's okay to ask me to do it."

Stepping forward, he ran his thumb along her jawline and nudged her chin higher. She became aware of how close they stood. His warmth enveloped her. The feel of his hand on her hip was both comforting and arousing, putting all sorts of unwanted thoughts into her head. And that curve to his lips was downright distracting. It made her dizzy, her thoughts woolly. She wondered what he'd do if she kissed him. And the ache to have his body cover hers became almost unbearable.

I'm lonely that's all.

"It's the perfect solution," piped up Edwina. "Free room and board for the lot of you but you'll be expected to work for it. I'll have no slackers in my house. Dodge and I plan to have Fig Tree Lodge up and running for the Christmas holiday-makers. All we need to do then, is work out how to get them to Bindarra Creek. And I know you're exactly the girl we've been waiting for."

"Mummy," pleaded Kaylee.

Dodge said softly, "Tessa."

On one hand, it was probably total madness to live under a copper's roof but on the other? Ian had once told her, living in plain sight can sometimes be the best way to hide. Plus, the alternatives in this run-down town were fairly dismal and Edwina was right, no place for a child. Feeling like she was about to leap from a perfectly good aeroplane with no parachute, Tessa mumbled, "Very well."

"Yay!" shrieked Kaylee, chasing Rufus around the table.

The look in Edwina Lette's eyes was both knowing and understanding. "You can enrol her in Bindarra Creek primary, so her school work won't suffer. That Maki man can make himself useful by cleaning out the old servants' quarters." She rubbed her hands gleefully.

"It's only for a few weeks," insisted Tessa, while her daughter and the dog ran out the door.

"A lot can happen in a day, let alone in a few weeks." Dodge brushed her fringe from her eyes. "Trust me. I know."

CHAPTER TEN

The days passed, settling into a familiar rhythm that soon had Tessa feeling she'd lived here forever. She'd sent the grant off as scheduled and had another meeting with the mayor which then meant the end of her responsibilities in that regard. She was free. No job waiting in Sydney for her. No monster from her past lurking in the darkness for there'd been no prank calls, no text messages, nothing. Gradually, she began to relax and let her guard down.

And the town waited to hear the verdict of the proposal.

On one level, she wanted the grant to be refused. If that happened, she couldn't leave. The money left in her account would probably only get her as far as the next town and two or three weeks' food and rent. And that didn't factor in the medication her daughter needed on a regular basis.

They'd have to stay. She'd wait on tables, perhaps start a yoga class, anything that would pay cash-in-hand and keep her off the books. They could find a small place to rent close-by to the school.

And no one would ever know she'd intended to steal these people's money even though the only thing she'd ever stolen before was a meat pie.

Dodge would never learn the truth about her...that she was a thief.

Wryly, she recognised it as a naïve dream because she'd always be on tenterhooks wondering when she'd be outed as a fraud. And when that happened, not only would Tessa be treated like a pariah but her daughter would suffer. Remaining here under their real names, also increased the likelihood they could be tracked down.

If only she'd never befriended that guy on Facebook. If only she'd never responded to his dinner request. If only she'd never thought it was time she put aside her grief for her young love and venture out into the dating scene.

Then, she'd never have to hide.

She couldn't go to the police. She had nothing concrete to go on apart from a few text messages and her childhood memories - too easily discounted by any smart lawyer. And if she did seek help from the authorities? She was positive she'd only fuel his rage and obsession. Every day it seemed there was a news story about some bloke who'd slipped his restraining order and attacked his victim.

No, she had to hope the grant would be approved. Perhaps she could pay the money back somehow? And there was always the option of staying on to administer the grant, living on the commission – and she couldn't deny how much the thought tempted. Perhaps she should wait a bit longer before making any hard decisions. They were safe here for the moment.

There'd been no more text messages.

No 'caller ID blocked' phone calls.

The problem was the longer she left it, the harder it would be to say goodbye.

On Wednesday, Dodge had arrived back at the Lodge early from work and built a tyre swing on the fig tree for Kaylee. Her daughter had given him a shy hug and the look on her face as she'd gazed up at him had spoken volumes. She was becoming too close to both him and his grandmother. It would be a painful wrench when they left and already Tessa was angsting over how her daughter would cope.

Maki had been right. Dodge was an honest man, a good man and so very kind. He had a quiet sex appeal that started every cell in her body humming every time she thought of him or he stepped into a room. And with every day that passed and every hour spent in Dodge's company, she began to realise she'd be leaving a good slice of her heart behind.

The following Friday night, they were gathered in the drawing room in front of the fire while outside the wind howled and rattled the windowpanes. Tessa had spent the week cleaning the remaining wallpaper off and readying the walls for the newly purchased paint. Her legs tucked under her where she sat in a squishy armchair, she experienced a sense of deep satisfaction as she studied the room. It would be magnificent once finished and a real draw-card for tourists.

But as Edwina had said earlier, how to get them to Bindarra Creek in the first place was the real problem.

Lou had already turned in for the night, claiming tiredness. Her face had been unusually pale and Tessa hoped everything was alright with her pregnancy. Although still reserved, Lou had begun to react in a friendlier manner around Tessa lately. But she spent a lot of time by herself and often Tessa would come across her, sitting on the front verandah as if waiting for someone. She'd wondered whether it was the father of her baby Lou waited for.

Across the room from Tessa, firelight flickered over Dodge where he sat hunched over a chessboard. Maki sat opposite sporting a smug smile and Tessa suspected he'd backed Dodge into a corner in the game. The game had become a nightly competition between the two men and one they appeared to enjoy immensely.

Maki will miss these chess games. Her old friend would accompany her when she left. Another one who would leave with regret. She turned a page in her book, not really registering the words. Over on the couch, Edwina, dressed in a lurid orange kaftan teamed with hot pink bunny slippers, was reading a Dummy's Guide to Japanese, a rug tucked over her legs. On the mat in front of the fire, Kaylee was sprawled beside the dog playing with her doll and the tiny stove Dodge had carved for her out of a piece of softwood.

It struck Tessa how much they looked like a real family.

The book fell from her shaking hands onto the floor with a thud causing Dodge to look over at her. He raised an eyebrow and asked softly, "Something wrong, Tessa?" His querying smile was warm, his eyes dark.

Nothing.

Everything.

Paper rustled as Edwina turned a page. Tessa desperately racked her brains for a coherent response and found it. "I've been thinking about how to get tourists into the town."

"Well done." Edwina tossed her book aside in a relieved way that made Tessa think she'd been hoping for a diversion. "What have you come up with? Oh wait a minute, while I get my pen and notebook."

Oh crap. Now what do I say?

"Dodge can build doll houses," Kaylee said.

"Actually," Tessa said slowly, her mind racing. "That's a good idea, sweetheart."

Kaylee beamed.

"Don't you think I've got enough to do? This house is nowhere near finished. Slave drivers." His grin as he moved his knight took the sting out of his words. He crowed to Maki, "Done and dusted."

Maki frowned, muttering under his breath. He leaned back and stroked his chin while he considered the board.

Stretching his arms in the air and smirking, Dodge worked out a few kinks. Tessa spent a lovely sixty seconds admiring his bulging pectorals and the sliver of stomach revealed when his long-sleeved, tee-shirt rode up.

Focus.

"Well," she began as Edwina sank back onto the lounge and waited pen poised in the air, an expectant look like a hungry bird on her face.

"Well?" Dodge grinned. His laughing eyes told her he'd rumbled to her ogling his lean body.

"Okay, I admit I haven't thought everything through but I do have one or two ideas. First off, I'd never heard of Bindarra Creek before I saw an advertisement in the paper." For the first time, Tessa wondered whether Edwina had had something to do with that ad. Tessa wouldn't put it past her. Advertising for young, single women to marry country boys would be right up her alley.

She eyed Edwina who stared back at her blandly. *Cunning old fox.* "We need to put this place on the map. It's all about visibility and the best way is through charity events."

Edwina sucked on the end of her pen. "What ad?"

"I'm not certain if I remember correctly. Perhaps it was a 'for sale' ad." Tessa raised her eyebrows when Edwina looked up and met her gaze.

Seemingly satisfied with Tessa's cautious response, Edwina stopped chewing her pen and wrote a few lines in her pad.

Tessa said, "Okay, moving on. The town could organize and hold some kind of charity event here. You choose a big-name charity, say for instance the Cancer Council, the Heart Foundation or Breast Cancer."

"We don't want to be giving away our money." Edwina snorted. "God, I could do with a smoke."

"Gran!"

Edwina waved her hand in the air. "Settle down boy, I'm being good."

Suppressing her grin, Tessa said, "These are only suggestions. Because a high-profile charity like these ones have such a wide appeal, you're automatically guaranteed press coverage. A few words in some TV day-time shows and you could potentially have hundreds, maybe thousands of people turning up on your doorstep."

"I've always wanted to organize a mud run," Edwina mused.

Tessa giggled as Dodge groaned. She added, "You could have more than one or building one event up to be really big by adding say photography contests, music festivals, food and wine festivals, that kind of thing. What do you think?"

"What about the doll houses?" Kaylee sat up and frowned.

"That could be a nice little side-line. You wouldn't need a shop only a web-page and you could build a range of doll-houses that would appeal from basic to the upper end of the market."

Kaylee hugged herself, her eyes sparkling with excitement. "Like a castle."

"I love it! These are fabulous ideas." Edwina scribbled furiously in her notebook. "We could round it off with a ball, one of those country bachelor do's to get things moving in the population department."

"Or a country and western night," inserted Dodge, a wide grin on his face.

Now it was Tessa's turn to groan. She'd discovered earlier in the week, his love of this genre of music when she'd heard him singing in the bathroom. If you could call it singing - the man was tone deaf.

But it was kinda cute.

"Chikushō!" Scowling, Maki picked up his queen and hovered above the board before replacing it back in the same spot.

"I've got you," Dodge said pointing at the board.

Maki muttered, "No, no. I must think."

"We could have pony rides," exclaimed Kaylee, who'd only that morning asked to go horse riding this weekend with a girl she'd met at school.

By dint of a lot of emailing and telephoning, Tessa had organised her to attend the local school for a while and had been quietly surprised at how eager her daughter had been to go.

"What a good idea, Kaylee. You too, Tessa. Florrie and the rest of the CWA are going to love it."

"What about a raw challenge?" Dodge quirked an eyebrow.

Oblivious to the conversation going on around him, Maki rose to his feet and paced the room before flopping back into his chair.

"I have no idea what that means." Tessa grimaced.

"It's kind of like a marathon mixed with an Army boot camp premise."

"Sounds horrible."

"No, listen." He leaned forward, hands linked together, his arms resting on his thighs, his earnest gaze holding hers. "People love it and we could organize two courses. One for the less physically able or more of a fun event and the other a bit more grueling for the serious minded. Gran could incorporate her mud run."

Tessa nibbled her fingernail. "Insurance could be an issue unless we get everyone to sign disclaimers."

"If we hold it over a few days, mix it in with some contests or the festival idea then round the whole thing off with a ball night, I'd say we could appeal to a lot of people. All proceeds, after expenses have been deducted, could go to one of those charities."

"Check mate." Maki plonked his queen onto the board and folded his arms over his chest.

Dodge swung back to the game and stared. "Bloody hell. I'm done. Again. You win mate."

Grinning, they shook hands across the table.

"I can't believe we didn't think of this ourselves." Edwina shook her head as she re-read her notes. "Your services are going to be in high demand, Tessa. Oh by the way, the CWA wants you to head the progress association once the grant comes through – we don't want Donaldson getting his hands on that money for his race course."

Feeling slightly stunned, Tessa could find nothing to say for a few seconds. The job would be perfect. If only she was staying here. She ducked her head and pulled at a loose thread in her jumper. When her mobile rang, she fished it out from where it had slid between the chair cushions with a mixture of relief and trepidation.

"I wasn't certain if I should call and mention it, Miss Gibson."

Tessa recognized the voice of Mrs McLean from the motel. Her ears pricked as she picked up on the underlying worry in the woman's flustered voice. Her smile fixed, Tessa rose from the chair and walked from the room, saying, "Mrs McLean, did I leave something at the motel?"

In the cold hallway, she leaned against the wall. Someone must have left a window open because it was freezing. Tessa clenched her jaw and hugged her waist with her other arm.

"No, no, dear. Are you missing anything?"

Tessa cleared her throat. "Sorry, I misunderstood. You were saying?"

"David, my husband, told me it's none of my business and probably doesn't mean anything anyway but then I thought and thought and really when it comes down to it if something happened and you lost your job because I didn't say anything, then really I'd be very cross with myself. As the good rector keeps telling us, be thoughtful toward your neighbours and lying really is a sin. Have you met our rector yet, Miss Gibson? He's a very spiritual man although I do feel his preoccupation with the church windows really goes beyond his calling. Now what was I saying?" Finally grinding to a halt, Mrs McLean paused.

"You called to tell me something."

"Oh yes. It was the phone call. When I think about it, no doubt it means nothing at all but I wouldn't want you go getting into trouble with your boss."

"My boss?" She'd been made redundant four weeks ago under the so-called government budget cut-backs. There was no way the head of the department she'd worked for would be calling her. Her fingers dug into the hard plastic of the phone. She felt as if all the air had been sucked out of her lungs.

"I don't think he left his name although he did say for me to tell you he called. He asked first if you were staying here and of course, I told him you'd been here and left. But when he wanted to know where you'd gone, I didn't feel right about giving him Edwina's number so I'm afraid I told him I wasn't certain. I know it was a lie but such a little one I didn't feel it would matter. Besides, I thought if you phoned him, you'd explain my position. David is always telling me how we should respect the privacy of our guests."

"Thank you, Mrs McLean." Tessa squeezed her eyes shut as if she could shut out the words going on and on, like striking fists.

"Then he asked me to give you a message."

Black spots swirled behind her closed eyes. Pressure built inside her chest until surely she thought she'd explode.

"He said to tell you, he'll see you soon."

And Tessa slid to the floor.

CHAPTER ELEVEN

Dodge knew he'd never forget that moment as long as he lived. The moment when he'd walked out of the drawing room and found Tessa huddled against the wall like a baby.

"Tessa!" He reached her side in two bounds, wrapped his arms around her and tenderly held her close. "What is it? Are you okay?"

A sob burst from her and she turned in his arms to bury her face in the curve of his neck. Her body shook so violently, his concern skyrocketed.

"Shit! Tell me what's happened. Are you hurt?" he demanded hoarsely, his heart slamming against his ribcage.

"I'm fine," she mumbled but he could feel his skin dampening from her tears. She clung tighter, her body shaking against his.

He rubbed her back for a few seconds before forcing out, "Is it bad news? Kaylee?"

"No. No. Everything's fine." She gave one final sniff then pulled away.

"Hey." Capturing her averted chin, he turned her face gently. "Talk to me. I'm here for you. Always."

She looked at him, her face drawn with whatever secret his gut warned she was keeping from him. Her dark eyes glistened with tears, her plump lips trembled. She blinked rapidly and hiccupped. "Sorry, I was just being silly. I guess this was a long time coming and when everyone was so happy and excited, I wished I could be here to see it all come to fruition."

"You can be here. Stay. You, Kaylee, Maki...hell the donkey too - you're all welcome to stay as long as you like." His lips twisted as he hesitated to say what was really in his heart. *It's too soon. You don't know this girl,* screamed his voice of caution. But he could no longer deny this girl had captured him body or soul. If only she could learn to trust him with whatever problem it was that caused that heartrendingly lost expression that crossed her face when she thought no one was looking.

Her lashes fluttered closed and he would have given anything to learn what she was thinking. "That's so sweet of you. I'll..." She moistened her lips and a different type of tension shot through his body. "I'll think about it. I promise."

When she looked up, nothing on this Earth could have stopped him from leaning closer and laying his lips against hers.

They quivered under his touch. They felt so soft and cushioning, like marshmallows, like he was sinking into their velvety sweetness.

He slid his hand around the back of her neck, feeling the silkiness of her hair cascading over his skin. Blood roared like floodwaters through his veins as he increased the pressure of his kiss. Her lips opened under his and hungrily he dipped his tongue inside. She met his rising passion with eagerness, her hands clenching over his shoulders and wriggling her body until she fit snug against him.

It felt like heaven. It felt like she belonged, right there, in his arms.

Groaning, he allowed his hands to roam up and down her body, relishing in the feel of her soft breasts under his palms, her well-toned bottom under the squeeze of his hands.

She kept kissing him, like he was the only man for her and his chest swelled with pride and awe. Her fingers danced along his shoulders, over his chest and lingered on his stomach where his muscles clenched and tightened.

The painful ache of his desire grew until he had to drag his lips from hers and whisper, "If we don't stop now, I'm not going to be able to."

Tessa giggled, a sound that delighted him.

Smiling he gazed into her flushed face. Her eyes were so dark he felt like he was falling into them, deeper and deeper.

"You're so beautiful," he said thickly.

She placed a butterfly-soft kiss against the edge of his mouth. "And you're the sexiest man I've ever seen."

He laughed.

"Dodge? What are you doing out there?" called Gran.

A huge smile spread over Tessa's face. "I bet she knows exactly what we're doing out here."

"Yeah." Dodge released the breath he hadn't known he'd been holding. "Sorry about that."

"I like her."

"I like you."

She searched his face, for what he didn't know but he hoped she found what she was looking for because he, sure as eggs were eggs, had. Gradually his heart settled into a steady rhythm again and she gently eased out of his arms. Shivering, her glance darted about the hallway in a way that made him wonder whether she was afraid.

"Are you busy later tonight?" She shot him a quick look then stared down at her hands.

He knew what she was asking. Heat flashed over his skin and his throat dried. He answered hoarsely, "I'll meet you down here, in the drawing room. Say nine to nine-thirty?"

Nodding, Tessa took his hand and he helped her to her feet. One hard hug and he let her go.

***

When they re-entered the drawing room, Edwina was on her mobile talking rapidly. From the gist of the conversation, Tessa understood she was being volunteered for organizing the charity event. She didn't care, in fact welcomed the extra work. She needed to keep her mind busy and off the chilling conversation she'd had with Mrs McLean. Besides, this type of challenge was exactly what she'd always dreamed of doing as a career. Instead she'd polished up on computer skills and typing and taken the first part-time job that was offered. A single mother with no family and a sickly baby had limited choices.

Edwina hung up and studied their faces with a casualness that didn't fool Tessa. She kept smiling pleasantly and willed her blush to blue blazes.

Tossing aside her rug, the old lady gave a massive yawn. "CWA meeting first thing Monday morning. We'll have a lot to do if we're to get this event happening this side of Christmas."

Tessa's eyebrows rose. "So soon?"

"No point in dilly-dallying about. Now, I'm off to bed. I'm bushed. Time you were in bed too, young lady."

Kaylee scrambled to her feet. "Can Rufus sleep in our room?"

"I don't see why not." Edwina held out her hand and Kaylee slipped hers into it. "Teeth and bed."

"Mummy, can you tell me a story?"

"Yes, sweetheart. I'll tidy up the tea things and be right up."

"I want the story of how Maki met Tails."

Rolling her eyes, Tessa grinned. "I must have told this a hundred times already."

"Pleeeeeease." Kaylee dropped Edwina's hand and rushed to Maki to give him a hug.

"Special dreams, Little Star," said Maki with a gentle smile.

Then Kaylee turned and shyly said, "Night Dodge."

"Night squirt." He crossed over and ruffled the top of her hair.

Kaylee giggled and ran from the room, calling to Rufus who took off after her in a mad scrabble of claws.

Taking care not to look at Dodge because she feared her longing would blaze like a neon sign on her face, Tessa wandered about the room picking up the empty cups and saucers.

Maki strolled up and said, "I will take walk, *Chan*."

"Goodnight, Maki." Tessa kissed his cheek.

He bowed and left the room. Seconds later, the front door could be heard closing and the clump of boots on the verandah then silence.

Over on the mantle, the clock ticked away the seconds. Tessa could feel Dodge's eyes on her and remembering their recent encounter, her fingers trembled making the china clink together as she walked into the kitchen. She made short work of tidying up and soon was drying her hands on the tea towel. She wanted to stop thinking about that phone call but couldn't. Not even the bliss of Dodge's kisses and the imprint of his strong arms enfolding her, could vanquish this nightmare.

Horror churned in her stomach and panicked-crazed thoughts spun through her mind.

How did he find me? Maki had sworn he hadn't been followed. Then how?

Everything will be okay. The dick is just messing with my head. Maybe if she kept telling herself that, she'd eventually believe it. But in the meantime, there was nothing stopping her making a call to a friend who worked for the government. Maybe a little pull of strings would see the grant proposal fast-tracked. Maybe the money could be in her bank account within a couple of weeks. Days even.

We have to leave here. I've got no choice. I won't let that evil bastard anywhere near my baby. Breathing quickly, she struggled to control her panic.

Dodge walked into the kitchen, leaned past her and closed an overhead cupboard door. The hungry glow in his eyes warmed her through to her bones. He kissed the side of her neck and murmured, "Later."

"Later," she promised and watched him leave the room. Tomorrow, she'd make that call. But tonight? She'd take and find what comfort she could in Dodge's arms.

***

Her heart beating fast, Tessa descended the stairs an hour or so later and entered the drawing room. Anticipation burned under her ribs as brightly as the flames of the fire Dodge was crouched beside, feeding with another log. His hair looked more tousled than normal as if he'd been raking it with his hands. A sign of nerves?

Could he be just as uncertain as she felt?

Her fingers curled involuntarily. On a primeval level, Tessa knew he wasn't a one-night stand type of guy. He oozed respect and a genuine liking for any female and the thought that he may see their taking their attraction to the next phase as a tacit commitment to something more permanent truly terrified her. She didn't want to hurt him. She liked him far too much to ever do that but neither could she walk away from what he offered.

Not yet.

He was like a rock or a steady immovable force that promised protection from whatever life chose to throw at her. If she'd met him under different circumstances, maybe even if he hadn't been a cop – she sensed they would have been good together.

She had a record – admittedly a juvenile one for petty crime but her association with Ian with his record of break and entry could very well paint a very different picture. How could a guy who wore his integrity like armour see past her youthful mistakes? How could he understand, she'd only been trying to survive? She'd never hurt anyone, never taken anything from anyone who couldn't spare the cash. And she'd only begged when she couldn't find work.

Would he feel different about her, if she told him?

Would it make a difference to him she'd been on the straight and narrow ever since she'd held her baby in her arms for the first time?

From that moment on, she'd resolved her little girl was going to have a different life. Her little girl was going to know what it was like to be loved and valued and to be safe. And then that gut-wrenching moment when the doctor had so very quietly told her Kaylee had been born with a hole in her heart.

She'd felt as if her baby was the one being punished for Tessa's sins and she'd thought she'd die herself from sheer agony.

But her daughter had survived the two necessary operations and here they were, living under a cop's roof on false pretenses.

She must have made a sound because Dodge looked around. The way his eyes lit up was like a fist in her chest. *Forgive me please, Dodge. One day, please forgive me.*

His smile was slow and sexy. Her body heated in instant response. He held out his hand and she hurried across the room to take it, loving how his grip was sure and strong.

"How's the little squirt? Asleep?"

"Yes. She wanted an extra-long story tonight."

"The one about Maki and Tails? One night, I'd like you to tell me that story."

"One night maybe I will," she whispered, fighting a sudden surge of choking emotion.

Rising to his feet, he tugged her forward until she nestled against him. He stroked his hands slowly up and down her spine until she relaxed. Her doubt over what she intended to do, fled. *He's a grown man. He knows nothing is written in stone.*

She lifted her head from his chest and pressed her thumb into the dimple visible in his left cheek. "I don't want to waste one second."

"Neither do I." His sudden grin was positively wicked. "But I also believe in taking it slow." He swung her into his arms and walked to a cushy armchair drawn close to the fire. Sitting down, he settled her on his lap.

Sighing, she hugged him close. His body was warm and hard and her curves seemed to fit into his angles, like they were meant to be just one and not two. She felt him press a kiss to the top of her hair and she smiled. Was there ever a man more caring than him?

His heartbeat was a reassuring thump beneath her hand, his body so strong and protective. If only she could stay here forever. While she'd been upstairs, he'd been busy. The room was lit by a lamp over in the far corner and the glow of the fire crackling and spitting in the fireplace. The double frosted doors leading into the formal dining room had been closed and the heavy brocade curtains drawn.

He'd set the scene for seduction.

And she was so ready for it. If he didn't make a move soon, she might well combust.

"Somehow I've gotten the impression it's only you, Kaylee and your Japanese friend," he murmured.

Tessa spread her hand over his chest where she could feel the rumble of his words still resonating. She nuzzled her face against the hard line of his neck and felt him swallow. "Are you going all cop on me?"

"No." He placed a finger under her chin and tilted her face up until she looked at him. "I'm going all man on you. I need to know if there's anyone else in your life."

"There's no one." She hesitated. What could it hurt to tell him a little about herself? "Kaylee's father died before she was born. In a street race. He was two years older than me but…" She smiled wryly. "He hung out with a rough crowd but I didn't want to have anything to do with them. When I fell pregnant he hoped to make some money out of the race for the baby. And then he died and Kaylee was born and she was so ill. I really didn't have time or the emotional energy for anyone else."

He nodded, like he got it and suddenly, Tessa realised he really did understand.

She asked, "What about you? Where does Lou fit into your life?"

His shout of laughter erased any further doubt in Tessa's mind regarding his relationship with his sergeant.

"She's a mate." His body moved beneath hers as he shrugged. "We look out for each other. I'm pretty bloody grateful she's been so accepting of me. My former work partner's been accused of dipping her fingers into what she shouldn't have and there's a few cops who either think I'm in on it or should have given her an alibi."

"Seriously? That's awful." Tessa's face heated and she frowned. "Are you saying you gave evidence against her?"

"Sara was guilty." His voice was unshakeable and the bottom fell away from Tessa's belly. If he could judge his ex-partner so summarily what would he do once he found out about her?

"She may have had a good reason for doing what she did," Tessa ventured in a small voice.

"Like what?"

Her gaze lowered to her lap and, picking viciously at a loose thread in her jumper, she mumbled, "I don't know. Sometimes life isn't black and white, Dodge."

But Dodge shook his head. "Doesn't matter. She broke the law. Anyway, if she had a problem, she should have come to me first."

"Maybe it was something she couldn't share. She may have been ashamed or frightened or didn't think you'd understand."

"I don't buy it. No, she crossed the line and almost took me with her."

Head whirling with so many confused thoughts and emotions, she didn't know what to think but before she could respond she realised Dodge was still speaking.

"...Bindarra Creek until the trial. It's taught me one thing, though." He paused.

Making an effort to sound normal, Tessa managed to whisper, "What's that?"

"I'm not so certain police work is the life for me. Until I'd come back here, I'd forgotten how much I enjoyed working with timber. I'd really like to try my hand at restoration."

Relax. Act normal. Enjoy this very special moment and forget about tomorrow. Tessa dug her fingernails sharply into her palms to regain focus. "Houses or furniture?"

"Both really."

"Then why don't you? I saw there's an antique shop in town simply screaming out for a makeover." She stopped plucking at the thread which was now quite long and cuddled closer, seeking the reassurance of the heat and the hardness of his toned body.

"You know, I never thought about that shop." Interest fired his tones making them deeper, darker and a shiver of awareness prickled her skin. "It could give me another source of income when I'm in-between houses. That's a great plan, Tess." He squeezed her tighter.

Problem is, I won't be here to see it. And I want to, I so very much want to. She shifted in his lap to face him and looked deep into his eyes, twinkling like stars. *Oh Dodge.* On the breath of a sigh, she pressed her lips to his.

He gathered her close, his breathing quickened, his kisses hard and hungry. Her body fired into tingling life. His hands roamed her body as thoroughly as a blind man, splintering the last whispers of her control. She twined her arms around his neck, dragging her fingers through his soft hair and shuddering when he scooped his hands under her buttocks, clenching hard. Desire melted her bones. His mouth left hers and he lapped his way along the side of her neck. She shivered, wriggling her bottom over the rigid bulge in his jeans. Her very core quivered when he sucked on the sensitive hollow at the base of her throat.

She wanted him.

He wanted her.

No more questions, no more maybes, only the here and the now. Tessa cast off all thoughts of tomorrow and surrendered to the ecstasy of his touch, whispering in his ear, "Time for bed."

CHAPTER TWELVE

At breakfast the next morning, Tessa realised she couldn't look Dodge in the eyes. If she did, she knew the memory of those wonderful couple of hours lying together would surge into her head. And she'd want to dive back into that glorious sea of pleasure and oblivion.

She knew he remembered every second, every detail.

Because heaven help her, so did she.

Looking relaxed in his woollen jumper and blue jeans and whistling tunelessly under his breath, he heaped porridge into his bowl and topped it up with cream. Every time he glanced at her, and she could feel that was often, there'd be this tiny smile at the corner of his lips. She knew because as soon as he looked away, her avid gaze would seek his face.

Everyone was in a good mood this morning.

And even better, there'd been no prank phone calls, no text messages with blocked ID's. Maybe he'd lost interest? Still riding on a desire infused cloud, Tessa clung, naively, to that straw of hope like she was on the Titanic.

The wind had dropped, the heavy frost forecast overnight had failed to materialize and the day promised to be mild with no chance of any chill factor.

Perfect.

"I think a picnic is in order," announced Dodge before shoveling a spoonful of porridge into this mouth.

"Mummy! A picnic! Where will we go?" Kaylee practically danced in her chair. Her eyes on Dodge, she imitated him with the porridge and Tessa gave inward thanks at this sign of the return of her appetite.

Glancing over at his grandmother, Dodge said, "Akuna National Park. It's not too far a drive and there's a great lookout over the western slopes of the Range."

Seated beside Dodge, Tessa frowned, wondering over the meaning behind that exchange of glances.

Under the table, he pressed his knee against hers. "You'll like it."

She blushed.

His grandmother's bright eyes sparkled with restrained mirth over the brim of her teacup. She took a noisy gulp before setting the cup back into the saucer with a loud clatter. "Let's do it then."

The following hour was a blur of noise and activity and it wasn't long before they were all piled in Dodge's Landrover. Even Maki had evinced interest, tendering a rare admission that he enjoyed dabbling in photography. A remark that had caused a deafening silence from Dodge and his grandmother for several minutes before that old lady had responded.

Tessa rode in the passenger seat alongside Dodge. In the back, her daughter was wedged in between Edwina and Maki. Kaylee enlivened the trip with her almost non-stop chatter as she leaned over to peer out alternate windows, exclaiming over the cows or the roos.

The road wound around open fields that gradually gave way to tree-filled paddocks before the road began to rise as they drove up the foothills and spurs of the Great Dividing Range. Outcrops of granite and rocky ridges scarred the earth. It was drier up here although the dusty-yellowing grass grew tall, especially close to the highway.

The car climbed steadily. At times, the road fell away on one side causing Tessa to gasp and grip the seat at the sight of the drop. Massive gorges rose before them with craggy cliffs from which clung intrepid grass trees. Above in the clear blue sky, a wedge-tail eagle soared.

Finally they turned off the bitumen and onto a dirt road where they bumped and jolted their way over a bone-jarring track that led through dense bush land. The road petered out into a large clearing of bottle-green grass and strategically placed shade trees. Three other cars were parked there but their occupants were nowhere to be seen.

The Landrover rolled to a stop. Dodge turned around and said, "This is the main camping area. There's a walking track that leads down to the river which is a great place to swim and fish in summer. There's another camping area further up the ranges. It's hard to get to unless you do some serious four-wheel driving. How about a walk to the lookout before we eat? There's something I'd like to show you."

"Sounds great. I need to stretch my legs." Tessa laughed.

Dodge opened his car door. "Be warned. This isn't an easy climb."

"I don't scare that easy."

"Kaylee, how about you and Gran go down to the river and feed the fish?"

"Okay." Kaylee scrambled out of the car and waited for Edwina to join her. They walked off, hand in hand with Edwina jauntily swinging a bag of old bread pieces.

Famous last words, Tessa admitted fifteen minutes later as she hauled her aching body over another outcrop of stone. Puffing, she pressed her hand to the stitch in her side and moaned, "When you said climb, I didn't take you literally."

"You need help, *Chan*?" called Maki from his position several metres ahead of both Tessa and Dodge.

"I'm good, Maki. Keep going."

"How old did you say this guy is?" Turning around, Dodge pretended to wipe sweat from his brow. He held his hand out to help her reach his side. "He's fitter than I am."

Tessa laughed. "I doubt it. I know you're holding back because of me. I do yoga and like to run but climbing a rock face? This is way out of my comfort zone."

"Actually, this is an easy track compared to some I've done and we don't need any special gear. I would never take an inexperienced climber where I normally go." Dodge shrugged. "I climb quite often to relieve stress. I was thinking of doing the Kokoda Trail one year."

"Yeah, well, you can have that one all to yourself. When I'm stressed, I meditate," she said wryly. "How much further? My calves are killing me."

"Not long, darlin'. This is the hardest bit." He hauled her close for a quick kiss and cuddle. "A bit of training with me by your side, and we'll conquer the Trail together. How about next year?"

Her heart skipped a beat. His smile was downright intoxicating, blurring her logic and obliterating her plans. "We'll see," she said weakly allowing her hand to remain nestled in his as they walked up the last steep section of track.

They rounded a large granite boulder and Tessa gasped. They stood on a smooth rock outcrop that jutted out from the cliff face and the view was spectacular. In the distance, she could see the hills and slopes tapering off to plains that stretched to the horizon. Below, the river snaked through an impressive gorge to disappear into thick bushland.

A neck-high cyclone fence had been concreted into the ground well back from the crumbling edges – a grim warning that no one could survive a fall from this height. Over to one side, was a timber bench where an older couple sat fanning themselves and gulping down water from their canteens. Close to the fence, a woman with short black hair stood with her back to them looking out over the valley. Maki was already lining up shots with his digital SLR camera.

Dodge swung her hand. "Not bad, hey, Tessa?"

"It's magnificent."

"This is what a wanted to show you." He looked at her and her heart did a free fall at the serious expression in his eyes. "My mother died up here. She was an amateur photographer.

When we were camping out by the river one school holidays, she came up here one morning by herself. By the time dad and I found her, it was too late. Snake bite."

The pain in his voice was still raw and touched her heart far more than she'd expected. She wanted so badly to take it away. "Oh, Dodge, I'm so sorry." It touched her to the core that he wanted to share this tragic and yet special place with her. Tessa laid her free hand against his face and he turned into her touch, pressing a kiss to her palm.

A simple gesture and yet it caused tears to well behind her eyes.

At the sound of their voices, the woman looked around.

The hand holding hers squeezed painfully and Tessa felt her fingers grow numb.

"Sara," Dodge said.

***

As far as picnics went, Dodge figured this would have to stand out as one of the worst ones he'd ever been on. The last person he'd expected to see turn up in his own back yard, was his ex-partner. And yet, here she was, as large as life and sitting in his grandmother's kitchen, looking unperturbed and drinking black coffee.

Her poison of choice.

While he downed his second scotch for the night.

He'd have to be deaf, dumb and blind not to notice the hostility simmering between Tessa and Sara. Although, Tessa didn't have anything to worry about - he'd never had the remotest romantic interest in Sara. But he hadn't had five seconds alone with Tessa to explain. Since that moment when they'd found Sara at the lookout, his ex-partner had been super-glued to his side. All afternoon, every time he stood or walked off somewhere, there she was following closer than his shadow.

It was weird.

He couldn't work out what the devil she was doing here.

To top it off, Lou appeared to have joined forces with Tessa and was acting like she was some kind of human shield, defending Tessa from God-only-knew-what and spearing him with malevolent looks. Maki had disappeared the moment, they'd arrived home. Dodge would have given anything to have escaped with him.

Kaylee had become over tired and sulky. Acting out probably in response to the adults' tension. Tessa had ended up wrapping her in a blanket and settling her in front of the television with a kid's DVD.

Maybe he should join her.

Glumly, he stared into his drink and rubbed his throbbing head. From the corner of his eye, he watched Gran pour the remains of her tea into a saucer. Any second now and she'd start her hocus-pocus. Normally, he'd laugh and join in her fun. But not today.

Not with the storm he sensed was about to be unleashed over his head.

"Well, strike me down with a feather. Are you going to ask her Dodge?" Lou slammed her hand down onto the table with a suddenness that made him start. Scotch sloshed over the sides of his glass. "If you won't, then I will. What the hell are you doing here, Pyeon?"

"I want some time alone with Dodge." His ex-partner's eyes flashed.

"No way." Suddenly Lou gasped and bent over in her chair causing both Tessa and Gran to shoot quick glances at her.

"Is everything okay, Lou?" asked Tessa, frowning. Her gaze dropped to Lou's protruding belly.

Bloody hell! The baby!

Looking up at them, Lou smiled. "It's kicking like it's going for the World Cup."

"Has to be a boy then." Dodge grinned.

"Yes and no," intoned Gran where she almost had her nose buried in her cup while she studied the leaves.

Across the table, Tessa met his eyes and bit her lip to hide the smile tugging at the corners of her mouth. Some of the tightness cramping his chest eased.

"I have to speak to you, Dodge. It's private." Desperation rang loud in Sara's high-pitched tones.

Dodge shook his head and Lou closed her mouth against another barrage of words.

"Whatever you need to say to me, Sara, you can say in front of them. They're family," Dodge said firmly.

Sara looked Tessa up and down, sniffed, then turning her shoulder to those on that side of the table, she addressed Dodge. "You have to help me."

"I'm not the one facing charges of corruption. Hell, Sara, you almost brought me down with you. You ruined my career."

Tessa reached across the table and laid her hand over his.

"That wasn't my doing. I never intended to involve you." Sara shook her head violently. Her dark eyes glistened wetly. "First off, you have to know I'm breaching the conditions of my bail by being here."

Dodge groaned, shutting his eyes. *Great, just great.* Through his teeth, he gritted, "You've now involved me even more in your shit and probably compromised anything I say at your hearing. I should get on that phone and turn you in."

"I had to risk it. Please, Dodge, hear me out."

"Why not give her a chance? Listen to her, since she's here."

Opening his eyes, he stared at Tessa. There was an expression on her face he couldn't interpret. Yearning? Wistfulness? Before he could pin it down, it vanished. He slumped back in his chair and said, "Hell yeah, why not. Go on, spill."

Sara spoke fast, as if eager to get it all out there into the open. "My parents are sick. They have no pension, no super, no one but me. When they come, sorry, came to this country already they were old and had to start with nothing. They worked hard but they had little education and found it difficult to learn a new language. Then they had me. Their miracle baby at a time when they thought they'd never conceive."

She pressed the palms of her hands to her eyes. "They needed private care but the housing market tanked and their house wouldn't sell. I became desperate. No bank would lend me money. I had no assets, all my savings were going in paying for a nurse to take care of them while I was at work. I asked myself, why not take the money lying in the Evidence? Why not use it? Get care for my parents. No one would know. As soon as the market improved, I'd sell the house and repay it all back."

"How long was this going on for? How much did you take? You could have come to me. I would have helped you somehow." He made no effort to dilute the fury surging through him.

Sara flinched. "On your wage? You earned the same as me and living in Sydney takes a big chunk of it. Besides, I was ashamed of my parents. I didn't want anyone to know what they were like." She paused then whispered, "Now, I am ashamed of myself."

"All of us here, at this table, are guilty of doing the wrong thing for the right reasons." Gran frowned heavily into her cup.

Her cheeks pale, Tessa withdrew her hand. Lou stared blankly dead ahead, her mouth a tight line.

Bloody hell. Dodge looked from one face to the other. Was there something else going on, that he should know about?

Deeply troubled over the undercurrents he sensed swirling about the table, he took another mouthful of scotch. It hit his stomach like a bag of rocks. Wiping his mouth with the back of his hand, he pushed the half-full glass away. He'd had enough.

"You want something from me, what is it?" he said flatly. Sara's admission worried away at the back of his mind. What did it remind him of?

"It'll be your testimony they'll use to hang me out to dry. I'll get twenty years and meanwhile my parents will probably die, alone, lost, thinking I've abandoned them," Sara said.

"You should have thought of that before."

Sara's voice rose. "Yeah, maybe I should have, maybe I shouldn't have relied on my partner not to dish on me."

"I had no choice," Dodge shouted, slapping his hands hard on the table. "Shit. I didn't know what was going on, only what I saw. You, placing a wad of money into your handbag after being alone in the Evidence. The next thing I know, I'm hauled in front of the Commissioner and hearing the sound of my career being flushed down the toilet. I was lucky they didn't believe I was involved."

"That's where you're wrong, Dodge." Sara reached over but Dodge evaded her outstretched hands. "They think you were in on it, too. Your lawyer convinced them not to charge you on lack of evidence. For the moment."

"I don't believe you."

"You have to believe me because sooner rather than later, they're going to come right back here and knock on your door."

"But why would they?"

Black eyes fierce, Sara ground out, "Because there's a shit load of money missing that I didn't take."

CHAPTER THIRTEEN

The headache Tessa went to bed with was still there when she opened her eyes early next morning. They'd all sought refuge in their rooms after Sara Pyeon's shocking announcement. She'd been given the sofa in the drawing room to bunk out on, the remaining bedrooms being uninhabitable. Uncertain whether or not to stay behind in the kitchen with Dodge, Tessa had decided her daughter needed her more. Besides, Dodge had his grandmother and Lou. Both of whom knew him far better than she did.

She'd found Kaylee curled up under the blanket and crying and was glad she'd made her daughter her choice. Shouting and raised voices had always upset her. So she'd shooed Kaylee up to their room and spent a little time brushing her hair and calming her down. After her daughter had fallen asleep, Tessa had sat in the little chair looking out the window into the night sky. Thinking about Dodge and the mess his ex-partner appeared to have immersed him in, about his grandmother's innuendo about people doing the wrong things, about how wonderful her life might have been if she'd met Dodge in another time, another place.

And she was another person.

And also, how ironic that his partner should be involved in fraud when that was exactly what Tessa intended to do, too.

Take money from a community that needed it desperately.

What kind of a person did that make her?

She definitely wasn't any better than Sara. And if Dodge ever found out... Heart heavy, her spirits low she raised herself on her elbow and gazed at her sleeping child for several minutes. Her hand shaking, she brushed tendrils of curly hair from Kaylee's face. So sweet, so innocent, so vulnerable.

Eventually, she eased out from under the covers without disturbing Kaylee and went to the window where she pulled aside the curtains and stared out over the frost covered scene. Wisps of fog drifted through the branches of the trees, obscuring her vision of the town that lay quiet and sleeping. And like her child, just as vulnerable.

The curtains billowed out suddenly and Tessa shivered as the temperature in the room dropped.

I can't do this anymore.

The import of that acknowledgement sent her sagging against the window pane. Her hands pressed against the chilly glass for purchase but it didn't stop her slide all the way down to the ground. Huddled in a ball, she rocked back and forth, back and forth, soundless sobs tearing her apart inside. Grief was like granite sitting on her chest, crushing the life from her soul.

But it was no use. She couldn't take from a community that had embraced her like she was one of their own. And one that was struggling to survive.

I'll find another way to keep my baby safe.
Somehow, I'll find it.

She crawled across the floor to her briefcase and unzipped her laptop from its case. In a matter of seconds she was connected to the internet and on the government site where she logged in her password. The grant proposal popped up – still pending. Quickly, she found the section detailing the bank account details and changed the authorised signatory from her name to the rector's wife, Mrs Florence Miller.

Her finger hovered over the enter key. As soon as she pressed it, the elaborate plan she'd concocted so reluctantly was over. She'd have no more reason to stay in this town and in fact, every reason to run as fast and as soon as possible. Before anyone found out the kind of person she really was.

Her hand shook.

Her entire body shook.

I'm sorry, baby. Tessa stared with blurry eyes at the small bundle under the doona and pressed the key. She put away her laptop and scrubbing her eyes with the backs of her hands stumbled off to shower and change. Her normal yoga routine would have to wait. It was time she reached out. Dressed in black leggings and a woolly jumper and socks, she headed downstairs to the kitchen.

Upon entering, her eyes immediately gravitated to Dodge leaning on the sink and staring out the window. No one else was around.

He turned and smiled but she could see by the dark smudges beneath his eyes he'd had an uneasy night.

"I missed you," he said as he crossed the room to draw her into his arms. His face pressed against her hair and he sighed.

Tessa snuggled against his chest, enjoying the heat of his body. *I missed you, too.* But she didn't say the words out loud. There was this hard lump clogging her throat she just couldn't seem to get past. Besides, an admission of how much he'd come to mean to her, would be tantamount to a declaration of commitment. That was something she wasn't certain she had the courage to do. Or the intention of staying.

Dodge eased her out of his arms. When she looked into his face, she found it shuttered, his normally sparkling hazel eyes flat, cop-like and her heart cracked.

"Coffee? Tea?" He turned from her and walked over to the cupboards where he flicked on the jug.

"Coffee, please." Her voice was so croaky, it didn't sound like it belonged to her. Wiping her sweaty palms over her thighs, she took a few shaky steps forward. "Dodge?"

"Yeah." He stood with his back to her, shoulders rigid.

She'd hurt him with her failure to reciprocate and she didn't blame him for his instant withdrawal. Yesterday must have been hard for him. He'd taken her to the very spot where his mother had died, he'd shared that painful memory with her. Maybe it was about time, she shared something with him. Maybe, it was time she opened up about her life and the nightmare that had twisted every decision she'd made since.

And maybe, one day, he'd understand.

But could he ever forgive her?

Her desperate intention burned in her gut like corrosion.

"How's Sara?" she began.

He shrugged. "Sleeping, I guess."

What if he could help her? She eyed his stiff back and twisted her trembling fingers together. "What are you going to do?"

Lowering his head, Dodge braced his hands on the bench. "Stuffed if I know. I'm not going to make that call though and dob her in that she's here."

"You could contact your lawyer straight away. See if he can launch his own inquiry into the missing money. Maybe he could find out exactly where the police are up to in their investigations."

"Yeah, I guess that's a good start." He turned and leaning back against the cupboard folding his arms over his chests. For the first time, she registered he wore khaki work clothes emblazoned with safety stripes.

She indicated his clothes. "Going somewhere?"

"Firewood run. Some of the local boys and me do this every so often. We go out to the bush and chop up the fallen trees and distribute it to the people in town who need it."

Her pride in him filled her chest to bursting. Eyes welling, she rushed to his side and laid her right hand against his face. "You're such a good man."

His cheeks reddened. "A bunch of us do it, I'm not the only one," he said gruffly.

"But you're the only one I care about."

His dimples appeared. Heat blazed in his eyes. "Just as well." He leaned in for a kiss and she closed her eyes for a few seconds, loving the pressure of his lips on hers. It was a gentle kiss, a tender kiss and for some reason, she wanted to cry.

"Tessa." Her name on his lips was like a vow.

It was now, or never. She stepped away and gripped her hands together. Taking a deep breath, she said, "My mother was a drug addict."

"That's tough." His tone was non-judgmental, the warmth in his face undimmed.

"I've no idea who my father was and I don't care." She gave a jerky shrug. "We moved around a lot. My mother's addiction became steadily worse and she would do anything to get her fix. I never knew half the names of the different blokes that came and went in our lives. But there was this guy...this one guy..." her voice shook.

Dodge went to go to her but she held him off with a raised hand. "No, please don't or I won't be able to continue." She gripped her hands together again as if by doing so, she'd be able to hold onto the control over her emotions she could feel was rapidly diminishing, second by second. "He hung around a lot. Kept coming back. I was pretty young but growing up fast and I soon figured out it was me he was interested in."

Dodge sucked in a sharp breath.

"He began to smack me around a bit, push me over, call me names, that kind of thing. And all the time, my mother would be lost in her lah-lah land totally oblivious. He'd say dirty stuff to me and tell me all these horrible things he wanted to do to me. I was terrified that one day he'd make good on his promises. And one day, he tried."

She rubbed the hot tears from her eyes. "I came home from school and found my mother unconscious on the floor. I couldn't wake her up. I called her name over and over. I even threw water on her face. Nothing. Then he walked out of the bedroom, stark naked and you know..." She gestured with her hands toward Dodge's groin and he nodded, his eyes going dark.

"There was this look on his face. I thought I was staring at the devil. In his hand, he held a syringe. He said he was going to make me happy. I panicked. I chucked my backpack at him and it hit him in the face. I guess it pissed him off, big time."

Tessa gave a nervous laugh. "He started shouting and saying how I belonged to him and he'd never let me go. He ran toward me and I ran into the kitchen and grabbed a knife. I used it." She pressed her shaking hands to her mouth. "I slashed the bastard across his arms and I think I got his chest too. There was blood everywhere. He used a tea towel to wrestle the knife from me. I thought I was going to die. I grabbed the jug and smashed him in the head. Luckily I've always been tall. He fell to the floor. I raced to my bedroom and grabbed my bag. We always had a bag packed for emergency get-aways."

"The only good thing my mother taught me." Her mouth twisted. "I tried to make her wake up but I couldn't and all the time, I was thinking, he's coming...he's coming." Her voice dropped to a whisper. "So I ran. I left her there. I never went back. And then two days later, I heard on the news there was a fire in our block of flats and she was dead."

Dodge cupped her face in his hands. "That wasn't your fault. Never your fault. You poor baby." He rained tender kisses over her forehead before pressing a kiss to her lips. "That explains a lot about you, Tessa. You don't know how much it means to me that you've trusted me enough to share what happened."

Then in his cop voice, he said, "Did they find him? Was he charged?"

"I'd been taught not to trust anyone but I still went to the local station but they did nothing. They wouldn't believe me. He was a legit businessman in those days. I was just some hooker's kid." She shook from head to toe. "They talked about calling welfare, so I told them to forget it and left."

"Then he's still out there." His mouth thinned to a grim line as he stepped away and paced in a tight circle.

"He's looking for me," she admitted, the words feeling like filth in her mouth. "Almost three months ago, I went on a date with a guy I'd met on line. I thought I was meeting a thirty three year old, real estate salesman with blond hair. Instead..." Her hands fisted. "Apparently, he came across my Facebook profile and recognized me. He set up a false profile and friended me. When I saw him...everything came rushing back. I had to get away. I got up and ran."

"He can be charged with stalking, harassment," said Dodge through his teeth, the pulse at the side of his mouth ticking furiously.

But Tessa shook her head, feeling close to breaking point. "How? I don't even know his real name. I just want him to leave us alone."

"That phone call." Dodge snapped his fingers. There was such fury in his face, Tessa stepped backwards.

Immediately, his expression softened. "I'm not angry with you and I'd never hurt you, Tess. I wish you'd told me though."

"I'm telling you now." Her mouth wobbled.

"Yeah, I guess you are. And I appreciate that." A self-deprecating smile spread over his face.

"Mrs McLean said a man rang from my work looking for me but I know that couldn't be true. It was him." Tears dripped down her cheeks and Dodge brushed them away with the pad of his thumb. "He's been phoning and texting me, too."

"Something else?" His voice was gentle, non-judgemental and her heart healed a little bit more.

"Yes. Oh, yes." She gulped. "It's not me he's after...it's Kaylee. He said...he said...he told me I don't interest him anymore, that I'm too old. I posted a picture of Kaylee at Christmas after her operation. Normally, I never put any photos of her up but I was so relieved the op was over, I just bloody well did it. It's my fault she's in danger."

Dodge drew a hoarse breath. "Bloody hell. Okay, this is what we're going to do. I still have one or two friends in the force, who believe in me. Actually, one is a kind of cousin. I'll get them to put some feelers out to track this bastard down and keep tabs on him. Once he's on a cop's radar, it shouldn't be long and he'll be hauled in for some wrong doing. The chances are a guy like that probably already has a criminal record. I'll take a formal statement from you and coupled with a full description and the names he's been using on social media - we'll catch him."

Tessa nodded. Somehow she didn't think it was going to be that easy, but it was a relief to know the burden of her terror was now shared.

Dodge held out his arms and she walked right into them, clinging tight. Never wanting to leave the shelter he offered.

CHAPTER FOURTEEN

Inside the police station, Dodge hunched his shoulders and blew on his stiff fingers to warm them while staring glumly at the cold fire-place. He wouldn't be there long enough to warrant starting a fire so the sooner he got cracking the better. After leaving home, he'd texted his mates saying he had business to attend to and would meet them in Snake Gully which was located in scrubland off the road to Boggabri.

First though, he intended to start the ball rolling where his girl's stalker was concerned. He smoothed out the paper on which Tessa had written her statement and re-read it one more time. His gut felt like it was crushed inside a giant fist at the thought of everything she'd gone through. And what she still might have to face.

But not if he had anything to do with it.

An hour later, he finally finished. Leaning back in his chair, he frowned as he considered the image on the screen. Taken ten years ago, the man staring blankly into the camera was one of three possibles his search had located. All three had used the name, Kevin Robinson, at various times. But this guy was the closest fit to Tessa's description. Under the name of Jason Taylor he'd been a wealthy property developer who'd crashed and burned when the market bottomed out. But changing your name wasn't a crime. At one stage, he'd been suspected of drug smuggling and hauled in for questioning after one of his many trips to Thailand but nothing had even been proved. Hence his meagre record. That part fitted in with Tessa's mother's addiction.

But as for an unhealthy predilection for little girls? There wasn't even a whisper of a hint in his file he'd ever been under observation in that area. He'd never done time. Never been charged. And under these two names, hadn't even received a parking ticket.

This may not be the guy.

Frustrated and angry with his inability to track down the perpetrator, Dodge roughly dragged a hand through his hair. He was missing something but what was it? And what the hell was niggling away at him? Something someone had said. But who? What?

Maybe Tessa had been mistaken in her memory. After all, it had been a long time ago and she'd been very young. Maybe he'd find the answer in her own record. The same one that had been niggling away at him ever since he'd found it. Before he was even aware of what he was doing, he'd dialed his cousin, Riley Morgan's number.

"Yo," came the sleepy response.

"Aren't you up yet?" Dodge asked. Cold sweat formed on his forehead. He hated what he was about to do. He felt like he was betraying Tessa's trust. He'd said her past was in her past and yet here he was scratching through it like a rat clawing through garbage.

"Geeze, Dodge, what time is it?"

"I've been up for hours."

"Ugh. Country boy," teased Riley.

With only less than two years separating them, Riley was the closest thing Dodge had to a brother although strictly speaking they were cousins several times removed. The connection was tenuous at best. After the Second World War, Dodge's great grandfather had married a cousin of Riley's great grandfather.

As school boys, Dodge and Riley had played together on the local football team, swam in the creek and dived in the river, explored the hills and rode horses and motor bikes over the Morgan property. And for different reasons, both had chosen the police force as their career.

"City dude." Dodge shifted the phone to his other hand and brought up another screen image. His pulse kicked up a beat as he said, "I need a favour. You remember that background check you ran for me?"

"Sure thing." Riley's voice was sharp, all cop.

"I need you to do a little more digging. I need to know exactly what was in the juvie record."

For thirty seconds all Dodge could hear was the sound of Riley breathing on the other end until he said, "It's already done and dusted, mate. I had a feeling you'd want to know so I did a little work on the sly."

Dodge's fingers dug into the hard plastic of the phone. "And?"

"Nothing major. Mostly kid stuff. A little shoplifting and a bit of street hustling, hardly worth the copper's time in processing. The street hustling was actually begging and the shoplifting was for a meat pie. I reckon the focus was really on the girl's boyfriend, one Ian born Ivanov Shivonoski, in and out of the foster system since the day he was born. That's why the girl was tagged and flagged. He was done when he was fourteen for a B&E, spent twelve months in Juvie and had a history of joy-riding in stolen cars. He had connections at the time with a gang that was suspected of performing a few armed robberies but there was never sufficient evidence to charge him. His file said he died in some street race. What's this all about?"

"Nothing much. Idle curiosity really."

Riley snorted. "That's crap and you know it."

"In the girl's file, was there any mention of...sexual abuse, a stalker or anything along those lines?"

"Mmm. Hang on a sec. I made some notes."

Dodge heard in the background a drawer being opened and the rifling of paper.

"Got it. I picked up a file notation some not-so-bright-spark made about the girl coming in and accusing a bloke of attacking her. She was nothing more than a kid at the time. The coppers didn't even bother to check it out."

Dodge exhaled slowly through his gritted teeth. "Is that it?"

"Sorry, mate. That's all I've got. You going to tell me what's up?"

Hearing the genuine concern in Riley's voice, Dodge gave a brief summary of the guy terrorising Tessa and her daughter.

"Shit, that's bad. You say you've made a report? Then I'll keep a close eye on everything or anything that pops."

"Thanks, Riley."

"No probs. Stay cool, Cuz."

"You too."

For several minutes after Riley rang off, Dodge stayed in the chair staring at the opposite wall at the faded Wanted posters. His damn cop radar was at full mast again. Thoughts, Riley's voice, Sara, Tessa telling him something, snippets of the reports Dodge had read swirled like a tornado through his mind.

There was a taste like sour beer fouling this mouth.

He hated this rising mistrust that was forming, hated how he couldn't stop remembering how each time Tessa had shared a snippet of her past with him he'd sensed there was more she wasn't telling him.

He'd known from the moment he met her, she was a complicated woman who didn't trust easily. And now that he'd learned more about her childhood, he understood.

But what was her secret?

What could be so terrible that she still hadn't told him?

She liked him. A lot. He knew that without one ounce of conceit rather like an acceptance that the sun rose in the morning. And he knew he'd fallen hard. Everything Riley had told him confirmed what he believed on a gut level – Tessa was a straight arrow. What she'd done to survive was peanuts and if she hadn't been tied in with Shivonoski, she'd never have been charged.

The thought of her, a child really, alone on the dark streets of a town that sometimes showed little mercy to the weak, horrified him. But she'd survived relatively unscathed, wary, sure but loyal and strong and loving. He knew with this girl, he wanted it all, wanted everything she could give him and that he'd do whatever he had to, to keep her and her daughter safe.

But crap it all, he also knew with a bone-deep certainty that somewhere in everything she'd told him, was hidden a lie.

And he intended to drag it out into the open.

***

After lunch, Sara departed in her car almost obscured by the cloud of blue smoke coming from the exhaust. The beat-up '96 Holden Commodore had definitely seen better days. There'd been such defeat on her face when she'd walked into the kitchen and said how she was going back to face the music, that Tessa had experienced a rush of empathy for the poor woman. Sure Sara had made bad choices but they were ones Tessa could fully understand. Desperation and fear could cloud your judgement so easily.

Dodge was still absent on his firewood run with his mates. Maki hadn't been seen since after breakfast. Tessa wondered, not for the first time, where in this small town he went every day. Surely he didn't spend all those hours checking on Tails?

Lou had gone to lie down in her room declaring how she didn't feel very well - a statement that had caused Tessa to check on her every half an hour much to the other woman's exasperation.

In fact, Tessa had been about to climb the stairs to Lou's tiny bedroom with a lunch tray when Sara had said she was leaving. She did her best to press Sara to wait until Dodge returned but his ex-partner was adamant. Sara did, however, ask Tessa to wish Dodge good luck and tell him how sorry she was for getting him involved. She appeared so eager, almost frantic, to leave that Tessa had wondered whether the woman was telling them the truth or whether there was more to her story than she'd divulged.

Then Tessa had had to deal with Lou who became emotional and wept all over Tessa's shoulder as she hugged her. Lou had muttered something about her fear of going parenthood alone, how the baby's father was a proper dick and how she didn't know what she was going to do after the baby was born.

Her actions were so out of character, it was all rather depressing.

Edwina, for once, kept her outspoken opinions to herself. She wandered about the house and garden all afternoon, mumbling under her breath one minute about dark shadows and the next, staring up at the overcast sky like she was searching for heaven. The entire time, Kaylee skipped along beside her, awe on her face as she gazed wide-eyed at Edwina like she was some kind of guru. Or prophet goddess.

It was enough to make any normal mother worry, let alone Tessa who wore her over-protectiveness of her daughter as obvious as a jacket. She ensured she was within eye-sight of Kaylee at all times. She wasn't certain if she was still on edge after dishing her dirt onto Dodge or whether it was the brooding atmosphere that seemed to have settled over the house since yesterday. One thing she did acknowledge, was a growing need to keep Kaylee close.

Lou finally emerged from her room around three and promptly took charge in the kitchen, whipping up enough food to feed a small army. Tessa left her alone and didn't go anywhere near that area, even when Dodge arrived home and instantly disappeared to help Lou without a glance in Tessa's direction.

She shrugged it off. *Let them play cooks and let off steam together.*

When Tessa walked into the drawing room, she squeezed her eyes shut in exasperation for a second. Edwina and Kaylee were sprawled in front of the fire poring over tarot cards.

Tessa marched over to what had become her favourite armchair and reached for the novel she'd left there on the cushions.

"Oh for pity's sake!" she hissed as she scrabbled under the cushions. She finally found the book wedged under the chair. She plonked down but didn't feel like reading anymore. A thought niggled away at the back of her mind, like she'd forgotten to do something but for the life of her, she couldn't figure out what it was.

I've got too much to think about. What with Dodge and that missing money and worrying over how I'm going to disappear. The only thing she was certain of, was that she and Kaylee needed to make tracks very soon.

Maybe whatever was bugging her had something to do with the proposed charity event. She decided then and there to plot out a plan of attack first thing tomorrow morning. The least she could do for this town, was lay the ground work for their first venture. She figured two days max and then Bindarra Creek would be nothing but an impossible dream for both her and her daughter.

Lou waddled into the room, Dodge at her heels and Tessa glanced over, welcoming the distraction of company. "What's for dinner?"

Averting her eyes from Tessa, Lou said, "Curry beef and vegies in the slow cooker."

"Nice." Tessa smiled at her.

Apart from nodding, Lou didn't respond. No doubt she was embarrassed at revealing her emotions to Tessa earlier in the day. That was cool with Tessa. She totally understood. Sharing was hard, especially if you were used to dealing with life on your own.

Dodge crossed the room and sat on the arm of her chair. "Lou tells me Sara's gone."

Tessa explained what had happened and relayed what his ex-partner had said.

Dodge rubbed a hand over his bristly chin and nodded. He leaned over and began to play with her hair, which she'd failed to braid that morning. "How you doing?"

Turning, she pressed a kiss to his wrist. "I'm okay." And smiled. Sensing eyes on her, she looked around the room.

Her face as hard as stone, Lou was rubbing her belly, like she was reminding Tessa of her pregnancy.

"Tessa..." began Dodge. There was an edge to his tones she didn't understand and when she glanced up into his face, his expression was severe.

Someone pounded on the front door and Tessa jumped. Dodge gripped her shoulder then rose to his feet and headed out the hall.

There was the murmur of voices then he walked back into the room, his eyes brimming with repressed mirth with no trace of his former seriousness. Those gorgeous dimples of his appeared as he attempted to hold back his grin. Coming straight to Tessa's side, he whispered, "Wait for it. You're going to love this."

Mrs Brown appeared in the doorway and stood there, bristling like an outraged hen.

Edwina looked up and waved her over. "Come in, Pam. Don't stand there like you're waiting for an invitation or hell will freeze over." Eyebrows raised, she tapped a card with her fingernail. "I knew you would come."

"For goodness sake, Edwina. Stop that idiotic nonsense." But she advanced to the sofa where she perched on the edge like a queen. Her razor sharp eyes swept the room to land on Tessa and they narrowed. "Right. There you are, miss. This is all your doing."

"I've got no idea what you're talking about," said Tessa, aware that Dodge was holding his sides and shaking.

"That man!" Pamela Brown spat. "That...that... foreign man."

"If you're talking about Maki, he is a naturalised Australian citizen." Tessa's voice rose. Kaylee sat up and stared at her. Tessa struggled to maintain calm. "He's probably more Aussie than you are."

"Oh, how dare you? You hussy."

"Hey. That's enough, Mrs Brown." No sign of any amusement from Dodge now, thought Tessa, inwardly hugging herself at how quickly he'd rushed to her defence.

Humming, Edwina patted her pockets and all eyes turned to her. She brought out a rolled up cigarette while Mrs Brown puffed up her chest, looking thoroughly outraged. Tessa stared. *Was that...?* But the old lady must have thought better of lighting up because she shoved it back into her pocket.

"A nice shot of vodka will set you right, Pam."

"You are impossible, Edwina. When will you learn to take life seriously?" Dismissing her life-long friend, Pamela Brown addressed Tessa. "You will take that man and leave this town immediately."

"Really? I don't think so." Tessa glared. *Actually we are leaving but not because you told us to.*

"Absolutely, you will because I will never, never agree to it. As long as God is my witness. Never!" Clutching at her chest, Mrs Brown's eyes rolled back in her head and she collapsed onto the lounge.

Edwina hooted with laughter.

"Bloody hell." Dodge bounded over, closely followed by Tessa. But they needn't have worried for the moment they reached her side, Mrs Brown had already re-covered.

Through slitted eyes she glared at her friend. "I can see you're full of sympathy as usual."

"Pwush. Get your head out of your butt, Pam and stop acting like you're on the stage. Maybe we should get the repertory theatre up and running again. Give you something else to think about apart from other people's business."

Legs trembling, Tessa sagged against Dodge who taking her weight sat on the lounge holding her on his lap. *Crazy old coot, scaring us like that.*

"How about you tell us what's got you so het up," said Dodge.

Pamela Brown pointed a shaking finger at Tessa. "I will never allow it, never! My sister and that foreigner intend to get married."

And on that note, a beaming Maki led Miss Beatrix Collins into the room.

Edwina sprang to her feet and shouted, "Champagne!"

Dodge clapped his hands. Lou put two fingers in her mouth and whistled while Kaylee chased the dog around the room. They were all as mad as one another.

Later that night after dinner and after Maki had driven a resigned Mrs Brown and his new fiancé home, Tessa bailed him up the moment he set foot back in the Lodge. She'd waited at the door with Kaylee and together they dragged him into the drawing room, where Edwina stared into the fire, Lou browsed a baby book on names and Dodge was pouring over renovation magazines.

Now with Kaylee gazing wide-eyed at their friend, Tessa felt almost just as breathless. It was like hearing first-hand about a true romance. The happiness shining in her old friend's eyes was so obvious it hurt.

"I want to hear exactly how it happened."

Maki ducked his head. "Tails bring us together."

"I knew it. She's a magic donkey," squealed Kaylee rushing over to hug Maki. "Tell us what happened, Maki *Chan*."

"The first day after we arrive, Tails escape from field and eats Beatrix strawberries."

Kaylee giggled and Maki ruffled her hair.

"I say I will pay, make amends. But Beatrix, so kind, so sweet, so..." His eyes glazed as he stared into the distance.

Tessa grinned. "Okay, we get that bit, Maki. Go *on*."

"You know she and her sister makes wine. Verily potent."

Tessa wondered what wine had to do with anything.

"Now, that I can attest to." Edwina waved a hand in the air. "Wheweee! Good stuff. I've told those two before, they should sell it."

"If the wine is that good, then that's a great idea. It'll give them an income." Tessa turned excitedly toward Maki who frowned. "What do you think, *Chan*?"

"You wish to hear story or not?"

"Sorry."

"They make wine from strawberries. Now all gone." He rolled his eyes.

"Tails is so greedy." Kaylee giggled behind her hands.

"I say I will do repairs to their house and work in their garden. And so it happens. I am a happy man." He met Tessa's gaze. "I will stay in Bindarra Creek."

The import of his words sank deep into her heart and her hands clenched. Maki deserved his chance at love and this new life. She wouldn't stand in his way.

But she would miss him every day of her life.

CHAPTER FIFTEEN

Early the next morning, Tessa typed furiously on her laptop as she worked out details of the charity event in a determined attempt to keep her mind off Dodge. Keeping one eye on the clock, she decided she had another thirty minutes before it was time to take Kaylee to school. Her fingers poised above the keyboard and she sighed. It was no use. She couldn't stop her thoughts from drifting to last night when he'd been about to say something to her before chaos had erupted in the form of the two elderly sisters and Maki. Then the moment had been lost.

She had managed a quick word amidst the celebrations and asked if he'd located her stalker. But he'd shaken his head. So whatever had him looking so sombre was something else. And the only thing Tessa could think it related to was he'd found out about her plan. Wanting to delay the inevitable, she'd kept her distance and did her best to avoid him for the remainder of the evening. She'd remained in her room doing a serious of prolonged stretches until she heard him leave the house.

Cowardly she knew but dreaded the moment when she saw the disgust in his eyes.

A high-pitched scream catapulted Tessa from her chair and sent her racing out of her bedroom and across the landing. Outside in the garden, Rufus launched into a volley of barking.

"Mummy!" Kaylee shouted. "Quickly!"

Her heartbeats so fierce they were painful, Tessa raced down the stairs two at a time, jumping the last four. Her socked feet skidding on the polished timber, she regained her balance and charged into the drawing room. Her gaze swept the room, searching frantically for her daughter. There she was – dressed in her school uniform and kneeling beside the crumpled figure of Edwina sprawled on the floor.

"What happened? Kaylee, are you hurt?"

"It's Gran, Mummy. She fell from the ladder." Kaylee pointed to where the ladder lay on its side and a paint tin leaked emerald green puddles.

That bloody ladder.

"Edwina. Edwina, can you hear me?" Tessa looked for blood, saw none and began to gently run her hands over the old lady's body for any obvious broken bones or swelling.

Edwina groaned and stirred. Holding a hand to her head, she attempted to sit up. "Ow! Shit a brick that hurt."

Kaylee gave a nervous giggle and Tessa spared another glance for her child. Cheeks too pale, eyes wide with fright she looked shaken but in one piece.

"Sweetheart, go and get the mobile from the charger in the kitchen."

Kaylee disappeared at a run.

"Edwina, can you tell me where you're hurt?" Tessa looped her arm around Edwina as she made another attempt to sit up.

Her face screwed up with pain, she succeeded. "My ankle."

Sure enough when Tessa lifted the hem of her trousers she spotted the ominous swelling. Blue and green bruising mingled with mottled red began to spread over the skin.

"Crap. You may have broken it."

"Crap is right, although personally I would have said something a lot stronger."

They looked at each other.

Tessa smiled wryly. "You already did."

"Ooops, sorry about that," Edwina said, rolling her eyes toward where Kaylee was running back into the room, mobile in hand.

"It's okay, forget about it." Tessa's voice rose. "But what were you thinking of? Dodge has warned you off climbing ladders."

"Everything would have been hunky dory if it weren't for Matilda."

"Huh?" Completely mystified, Tessa wondered whether Edwina may have experienced a blow to the head.

"You know, Mummy. The ghost." Kaylee offered the mobile.

"The ghost. Right."

"If you're thinking of dialing triple zero, forget about it. Oomph. Here help me straighten up a bit, girl."

Tessa assisted maneuvering Edwina onto a nearby chair where she subsided with another groan.

"I'm sorry, Gran." Kaylee's chin wobbled as a tear tracked down her cheek.

"Don't be silly, child. There's nothing to be sorry about, you startled me is all." Edwina patted Kaylee's hand.

"I still have no idea what happened. But we need to get you to a hospital. You need an x-ray and probably a good check-up to make sure you haven't injured yourself anywhere else."

"Pwush, Tessa. Settle down."

"I'm serious." Tessa waggled the phone in Edwina's face. "Hospital or I call Dodge. Your call."

"I'm trying to tell you, girl, the ambulance will take a good hour to get here. No need to fuss, you can drive me yourself to the doc's."

"You need an x-ray."

"Well, that ain't going to happen unless we get to Armidale. X-ray facilities are on our list for the poly-clinic upgrade."

Tessa remembered what Rhiannon Scott had told her about the lack of medical facilities in Bindarra Creek. *God, but this town needs more than a makeover.*

Bowing to the inevitable, she said, "Then Armidale it is. Kaylee, run and get both your hooded coat and Mummy's please. Oh and grab a blanket off the bed for Gran."

"You're not serious."

"Yes, I am." There was no way she was going to gamble with this wonderful if too determined old lady's health. "We're not taking any chances. I'll phone Dodge and let him know where we're going and leave a message for Maki."

"You're a good girl, Tessa." She leaned close and stared deeply into Tessa's eyes. "If only I could see the rainbows but those blasted shadows are too thick."

Tessa sighed. "Forget the psychic stuff, Edwina, unless you can wish yourself out of this house. Getting you into the car is not going to be easy."

"Anything worthwhile is never easy, girl. And don't you forget it. Come on then. Let's get this over with."

"I'll just fetch my bag and keys. I won't be a sec." She squeezed Edwina's hand which felt way too cold to the touch and hurried into the kitchen where she'd left her handbag on the counter after her early breakfast.

Hang on, it's not there. I'm certain, I put... Frowning, Tessa swept her gaze over the countertops and the table. *I must have been mistaken,* she thought as she spied her bag resting on one of the kitchen chairs. She swooped it up, dug inside and found a small notebook. After scribbling a quick message for Maki which she propped up against the fruit bowl, she let the still madly barking Rufus inside before pulling on her boots and returning to the drawing room.

Kaylee, her cheeks not quite so pale now, stood beside Edwina's chair, holding the items Tessa had demanded. Rufus sniffed and whined about her legs.

"Can you also carry mummy's handbag, sweetie?"

Kaylee nodded and Tessa added her bag to the pile.

Turning to Edwina, she said, "Ready."

Edwina braced her hands on the armchair while Tessa scooped an arm around her back and helped her to her feet. The old woman didn't make a sound as she hopped out to the house, leaning heavily on Tessa. When they reached the sedan, her face was chalk white and her breath was coming out harsh and quick.

"Do you need any pills?" Tessa asked in a low voice as she buckled Edwina into the passenger seat.

"Got them in my pocket but I'm fine for the moment. I'll settle as soon as I can rest up."

Tessa took the clothes off Kaylee and placed them on the back seat before tucking the blanket around the old woman. Turning around, she sighed when she saw her daughter had let the dog inside the car.

Kaylee's chin jutted mulishly. "Rufus wants to come, too. He's upset."

"I guess it doesn't matter." She leaned over and checked Kaylee's seat belt was done up tight, receiving a wet lick on the face for her troubles. "Lovely. Thanks Rufus. There, all done. Let's rock and roll."

Tessa started the engine and drove out of the yard while she quickly phoned Dodge and brought him up to speed. He immediately asked her to swing past the police station and pick him up on her way.

She flicked the left indicator and turned the car toward the station. "Well, Edwina, are you going to tell me what happened? Did you feel dizzy or something?"

"It was my fault," Kaylee said from the back seat, beginning to cry. "I'm sorry."

"I'm sure it wasn't your fault, sweetheart. Edwina should never have been on that ladder."

"While I've still got the use of my body, I intend to use it!" declared Edwina, huffily.

"But it *was* me, Mummy! I told Gran I saw Matilda and that she talks to me and Gran said, *'Fucking hell'* and fell onto the floor."

And Edwina laughed.

***

By the time they arrived back at Fig Tree Lodge, it was getting onto midnight. Clouds scudded across the sky and obscured the moon. With no streetlights and the house in darkness, the aura of isolation was intense.

Tessa shivered and couldn't stop herself from flicking an anxious look at the deep shadows surrounding the house.

Kaylee, Edwina, with her ankle in plaster up to her knee, and the dog were all sound asleep in the back seat. The car smelt like McDonalds, a late and quick-fix dinner on their return journey. Never a fan of fast food, the meal sat queasily in the bottom of Tessa's stomach. That plus the stress headache pulsing painfully behind her eyes, it was a wonder she managed to remain upright.

What a day.

Dodge switched off the engine. "Thanks for being there."

"Actually, if we hadn't been here, this probably would never have happened." Tessa turned around to gaze at the sleeping trio illuminated briefly by the overhead light. Unclipping her belt, she whispered, "Kaylee told your grandmother she saw a ghost. I'm afraid Edwina was so surprised she fell off the ladder."

"Gran believes Matilda is still hanging around the Lodge, trying to find her twin brother."

"What about you?"

"I've never seen her." In the darkness, she saw the movement of his shoulders lift in a shrug. "And you, Tessa? Have you seen her, heard her?" Amusement hummed briefly in his voice.

"No, thank heavens and I don't want to." Shuddering, she repressed the memory of all those times when inside Fig Tree Lodge, she'd felt a cold breeze flutter over her face. "Come on, let's get this lot to bed. I'm bushed."

"Okay, but then we need to talk."

The cool words so at variance with the warmth that had infused his voice these past few days, sent an icy trickle of warning down her spine. This was it – the moment of truth – she just knew it.

The moment when the light in his eyes for her would die.

***

"Sit down, Tessa, you look tired." Dodge indicated the couch with a sweep of his hand.

She shook her head. "I prefer to stand." Her hands balled into fists at her side. "Well, get on with it."

He studied her for so long, she could have screamed then said, "This isn't easy for me either you know."

Her false bravado crumbled. "I know."

"I'm pretty certain I've figured out why you're here." His lips twisted. "The pieces fell into place after Sara arrived and said how she couldn't talk to me because she was ashamed. I couldn't work out what her words reminded me of until eventually I remembered you'd said something similar. When I recalled the way you acted that night when we were discussing Sara's case, I had a pretty good idea that whatever you were up to was similar to what Sara had done. Then bingo. The grant money."

Tessa kept her head high. "I guess there's nothing left to say then."

"Bloody hell, Tess, you're not making this easy." One hand combing through his hair, the other shoved in his jeans pocket, he paced up and down in front of the fireplace.

"I don't have any excuse. I saw what I thought would be a solution to my problem and I took it."

His jaw worked as he stared at the wall, face averted like he couldn't bear to look at her. She didn't blame him. She couldn't look herself in the mirror either. "I know what you must think of me."

"Do you?"

"Sure." She spread her hands wide and tried to smile through the tears blinding her vision. "You're a good cop and I'm on the opposite side of the law. Do you intend to charge me?"

"Let's make this clear shall we? My guess is correct? You're here to de-fraud my town of the grant funds."

"That's it in a nutshell." Tessa shoved her trembling hands behind her back.

He pressed a hand to his eyes. The line of his shoulders was rigid with tension. "Since no money has yet to pass into your hands, I don't see that an actual crime has been committed."

She took one shaky step forward.

He turned his back.

"We'll leave as soon as possible." Her voice cracked. "If it's any consolation, Dodge, I couldn't go through with it. I hate myself for what I almost did to this town and wish I'd never embarked on this dumb idea. No matter which way I tried to justify it, in my heart I've always known what I was doing was wrong. I've already taken my name and my details off the proposal. The authorised signatory for dispersal of the money is Mrs Miller."

She felt it then, a savage ball of grief building up pressure in the core of her being and ran from the room. She wanted so badly to beg for forgiveness but equally she knew her actions had driven a wedge between them that could never be bridged.

Tomorrow. We'll leave Bindarra Creek tomorrow.

CHAPTER SIXTEEN

Later, Tessa swore Scout's honour, it was the touch of chilly fingers trailing down her face that woke her. Heart thudding, she gripped the throw rug and stared into the darkness. Something was there, in this very room.

Unable to sleep, she'd finally left her bedroom and trailed down to the kitchen where she'd spent who-knew-how-many hours staring out the window into the night. Eventually, she'd stumbled into the drawing room and collapsed on the couch, hugging the rug close to her ice-cold body. She felt hollow and drained like there was nothing left of her. All she had to cling to, was the love for her little girl and her need to see her safe.

She must have fallen asleep for she gained the sense that the time was somewhere around two or three hours before dawn.

Straining her eyes, she searched for anything out of place, a darker shadow that shouldn't exist. She listened. No sound. Nothing moved. There was nothing but the rapid thump of her heart.

I'm being paranoid.

But she couldn't shake the feeling something was terribly wrong. In the distance, a dog howled.

All her hairs stood on end.

A waft of ice-cold air swept over her face. Was there a window left open? Was that the reason for the freezing temperature inside the room? Or could it have a more sinister connotation?

Feeling more than a little silly, Tessa wiggled to the edge of the lounge and perched there. She whispered, "Matilda?"

There it was again.

That chilly touch, like the breath of something beyond the grave. This time on her bare arm.

Tessa sank her teeth into her bottom lip to stop them chattering and threw aside the throw rug. She glanced over at where the frosted-glass, double doors led into the hallway.

On the first floor, Dodge slept. Maybe she should rouse him and ask him to check the windows and doors. But the memory of the last words he'd spoken were still bitter in her mouth.

No need to wake him. She could imagine how idiotic she'd sound if she tried to explain. And he'd made it plain as day, he wanted nothing more to do with her. No, she'd go to the loo and back to the huge bed she shared with Kaylee.

She wrapped the throw rug around her shoulders and felt glad she was wearing flannelette pajamas. Only marginally warmer, she tiptoed, shivering and shaking to the door feeling as though the icy shadow moved with her.

She reached for the door handle. Her hand flayed in the darkness.

No doorknob.

No reassuringly solid timber under her touch.

Nothing but cold air.

Which could mean only one thing, the door stood open.

I know I shut it behind me when I came downstairs. Could someone else be inside the house? The terror that had haunted her for so long paralysed her limbs. Memories of what had happened crowded into her mind, shrieking like banshees. *This is just a dream. Just a dream,* she chanted while she stood in the doorway as if turned to stone.

Kaylee. The voice inside her head didn't belong to her.

It broke through her mind-numbing fear. Adrenaline coursed through her body and she launched into movement. She bounded up the stairs, ran along the landing, down the hallway, her breaths sobbing gasps, barely aware she screamed her daughter's name. At the other end of the house, Dodge shouted.

She grabbed the doorknob. It slipped through her damp hands.

Tried again. Turned the bloody thing while at the same time, ramming the door with her shoulder.

She staggered into the room. Her fingers slammed onto the wall and located the switch. Light glowed from the baroque light-fitting overhead. Her frantic gaze arrowed to the bed.

It was empty.

Her heart felt as if it splintered into a million pieces.

One of the French doors stood wide, the curtains pulled back. Dodge skidded to a halt behind her, his chest heaving. "What the hell's going on?"

"Kaylee. She's gone." *My baby. My baby.*

They rushed to the bed where Tessa flung blankets, doona and pillows onto the floor while Dodge crouched down and peered underneath.

"Nothing. What's that smell?" Dodge said, sniffing the air. "Smells like nail polish that's gone off."

Tessa whirled around. A crumpled white rag lay near the open door. She went to pick it up.

"Wait." Dodge grabbed her waist. "I think that's chloroform. Don't touch it. It could be evidence."

Evidence of what? "Kaylee. Kaylee." Tears streamed down Tessa's face while the knot in her stomach grew larger and larger.

"Check the bathroom. I'll check the verandah. Move, Tessa." He gave her a little push before hurrying across the bedroom while Tessa stumbled forward and went to run back down the hall.

That icy draft surrounded her again.

Could it mean something? Was Matilda here, trying to tell her where Kaylee had gone?

Tessa stepped forward.

The coldness swirled and ebbed around her.

Crap. I can't believe I'm trying to communicate to something that doesn't exist. But her daughter's life was at stake and she'd do anything, try anything to save her.

"Okay, Matilda, where is she?" Her heart beating fast, Tessa strained all her senses. She felt the icy shadow leave her side. She stepped forward toward the bathroom. Nothing. Turning around, she took one step toward the back of the house and where a narrow staircase, used decades ago by servants, led down to the laundry. And felt it. The coldness like a coating of snow on her skin.

This way.

She followed her instincts and crept as quietly as she could toward the old stairwell. Every step of the way that chill drifted by her side.

Dodge bellowed her name but she didn't dare respond in case she gave away her position.

He's here.

She could feel that bastard's tainted presence in the very air she breathed. Like something foul and truly evil.

She heard the thudding of footsteps and the raised voices of Lou, Edwina and Maki but she didn't stop. The barking of that dog sounded louder. It echoed faintly. Could it be Rufus? Was he locked up somewhere? He'd slept every night since they'd arrived in Fig Tree Lodge curled up in a dog bed in their bedroom but now Tessa remembered how he'd scratched at the kitchen door to go out just before she'd put Kaylee to bed.

Kaylee.

Oh God. My baby. Where are you sweetheart?

She reached the stairs and stared down into the well of darkness. Was that a movement? *Shit!* No, it was torchlight and by the way it bobbed and weaved, Tessa figured that someone was in the laundry, perhaps struggling with the old-fashioned bolt at the top of the door. Her right hand gripped the railing, as she began to creep step by step down the stairs.

The door opened with a whine.

NO. NO. NO.

If he had a car waiting outside, she may never catch him and her daughter would be lost forever. Tessa flung back her head and screamed, "He's outside. The back staircase."

She plunged down the remaining steps. Her feet slipped in the dark. She fell forward and tumbled the remaining four to land, bruised and aching at the bottom.

Pushing to her feet, she hurtled out the door and hesitated at the edge of the verandah, her breath wheezing in and out like a chain saw.

Which way? Which way?

The yard surrounding the house was thick with shadows from the tall trees and so still, she thought he'd hear the sound of her rapid breathing.

The dog was barking hysterically now. And definitely coming from the direction of the old servant quarters. *I'm sorry Rufus. You have to wait.*

Think.

If he had a car, he must have parked on the road or someone would have heard him coming up the drive.

She ran around the side of the house, heading for the driveway. Then stopped to listen. The wind stirred, rustling the leaves in the fig tree. She heard the far-away bellow of a cow. Nothing out of place.

And that strange coldness was no longer anywhere near her.

Wrong way. I've gone the wrong way.

Spinning around she raced back the way she'd come and cannoned into something solid and heavy.

"Tessa! Have you found her?" demanded Dodge.

"No. Dodge listen, is there a laneway or a track bordering this property?"

"Not really. But the doc has a small car park off to one side of his surgery. It's this way." Taking her hand, he led the way as they ran across the front lawn and through the gardens on the north side of the house. "I told Maki to look after Gran and Lou. Lou's on the phone calling reinforcements but it'll take them a while to get here."

"Okay," Tessa panted. The burn in her side seemed to cut through to her bones and she could no longer feel her feet from the frosty ground. But she didn't stop. She'd never stop until she had Kaylee in her arms again.

"I hear a car starting up." The desperation in Dodge's voice slashed through the remains of Tessa's heart.

Sobbing she followed him in blind faith, as Dodge swore then raced around a garden bed of thick bushes. Then the grass gave way to gravel that bit and stung her bare feet.

They'd reached the carpark.

And there ahead of them, was a pair of red tail lights moving rapidly away from them.

Dodge took off.

Tessa raced after him, her eyes fixed on the car. From somewhere down the road, another car engine revved.

Tyres spun on gravel. The tail lights in front of her bumped up and down. The car had crossed the gutter and was now on the Main Road.

Dodge had outpaced her but he was still nowhere close enough to stop the car.

I'm losing her!

The roar of another car thundered through the night. It sounded like it was almost on top of them. Headlights lit up the road and the next instant, the car slammed into the bastard's front passenger's side, ramming the car up against a telegraph pole.

Dodge reached the wreck, calling Kaylee's name. The headlights from the other car lit the scene. Smoke poured from the engine. The air stank of petrol and burning rubber. Tessa heard a door screech open. She saw the shadow of Dodge reaching in for her daughter. Saw the driver's side-door fling wide.

Saw *him!*

His face contorted with rage, he screamed as he dragged Dodge out of the car and hurled him to the ground.

Fury consumed her.

Tessa leapt the last metre, straight onto the bastard's back, yanked his head back by the hair with one hand, her fingers of the other, like claws going for his eyes. She screamed, "I'll kill you. I'll kill you."

He whirled around, slammed her against the side of the car. Pain shot down her back. Her grip loosened and she fell.

But Dodge was on him, smashing a fist into his face, pounding another into his gut. They laid into each other, the thuds of hands pounding into flesh sickening.

"Mummy," whimpered Kaylee.

"I'm here." Tessa staggered to her feet and hanging onto the side of the car, leaned inside and smelt the stench of fresh vomit. "Sweetheart, can you move?"

"I think so. I've been sick."

"Kaylee. You need to take my hand and get out of the car."

"I'm scared, Mummy."

"I know sweetheart. Come on. Can you see my hand?"

Small, cold fingers found her hand and clutched tight. Tessa tugged her daughter forward until she'd appeared out of the shadows. "Kaylee." She forced back the sobs wracking her chest, as she gazed into her daughter's tear stained face. "Come on, out you get."

"She's mine!" snarled the voice from her nightmares. Cruel hands pulled her away.

Tessa staggered around and fought back, kicking and screaming. Her knee connected with something soft and he howled.

"Run, Kaylee. Get out the other side. *Run.*"

Dodge. Where was Dodge?

"You never should have left me, Tessa. You've been a very naughty girl." He was there. Standing in front of her. "You need to be punished taking her from me."

"How did you find us?"

"I merely phoned every hotel, motel and pub in NSW. Lucky me, the motel you stayed at was near the top of the list." Light glinted off the knife held in his hand, as he slashed it through the air. Back and forth. Back and forth. "Remember this?"

Shit, could it be the same knife she'd used on him all those years ago? Her heart stuttered.

Blood dripped from the blade.

Dodge. Oh, Dodge.

Slowly, she raised her chin. Stared at him. Blocking his passage into the car with her body. Willing Kaylee to obey and run. A car door creaked open. Unbelievably, she heard Sara's voice urging Kaylee to get out of the car. *Thank you, Sara. Run.*

A shadow rose up out of the darkness and stepped into the pool of light. *Dodge!* He crashed the wheel-jack against the guy's spine. The bastard crumpled, attempted to rise to his feet.

Dropping his weapon, Dodge staggered forward and with an upper-cut right into his chin, laid her nightmare out cold on the ground.

"Kaylee?" asked Dodge, voice hoarse with dread.

"She's okay. She's been sick but she's okay. Sara has her." Tessa burst into heaving sobs.

"Thank God. Oh, Tessa darlin', I thought I lost you. Lost both of you." Dodge dragged her into his arms, kissing her hair, her nose, the side of her face for one wild thirty seconds before looping an arm around her shoulders. Together, they staggered around the remains of the car and saw Kaylee standing with her hand in Sara's at the corner of the road.

Torchlight bobbed toward them.

Men shouted and yelled.

They could have been aliens as far as Tessa was concerned. She dropped Dodge's hand. As Tessa ran toward Kaylee, all she could see was her beloved daughter - her thin arms outstretched and smiling through her tears.

CHAPTER SEVENTEEN

The morning had come and gone and now it was mid-afternoon. But time was a blur for Tessa. Questions and more questions from what seemed like a never ending parade of people who tramped into Fig Tree Lodge and demanded answers.

A police Task Force had arrived to secure the scene and take the injured perp under guard to Armidale hospital. They'd spent some considerable time grilling Tessa and taking her statement and the way their hard, flat eyes had drilled into her had frightened her. Since they didn't ask what she was doing in Bindarra Creek, she kept quiet about her initial intentions. But had Dodge told them? Any moment, would they return and drag her away in handcuffs? Then what would happen to Kaylee?

Blindsided by her collision with her past, she'd not only risked her own life but her daughter's future. It was time she started trusting others and trusting the system and

Tessa vowed she'd never make the same mistake again.

The townspeople had been wonderful. Many had arrived bearing platters of food, cartons of beer and Mrs Brown had turned up with what she declared to be her best laying hen.

Doc Warner with Rhiannon Scott in tow, had been one of the first to be allowed entry and he'd given all of them a thorough examination. Dodge was first up, considering he was bleeding from a stab wound to his back. But luckily it wasn't too deep and only required a few stitches. Tessa had then insisted her daughter be examined and after declaring Kaylee to be perfectly fine, he'd looked Tessa over, tutting at the cuts on her swollen feet and the bruising now presenting itself in a myriad of colours all over her body from her fall down the stairs. He prescribed rest for all of them and pain killers for Tessa who, by that time, felt like she could have swallowed the entire box. She was positive there wasn't one bit of her body that didn't ache.

She'd done her best to fade into the background but instead found herself and Kaylee centre stage as the community offered their sympathy and best wishes. It all only served to make her feel even worse about herself. These were good people who'd given her friendship and in return, she'd been prepared to leave them wanting.

She dreaded the moment when Dodge told all and sundry what she'd been up to, but so far, he'd remained quiet, his face inscrutable every time she dared to look his way.

When Tessa mentioned it was a ghost that had warned her, no one but Edwina and Kaylee believed her. She'd picked over the lunch a pale-faced Lou had made for her but her appetite had fled. She'd come so close to losing Kaylee, she couldn't stop shaking. Those insane minutes when Dodge and she had fought that madman kept replaying over and over inside her head. The moment when she'd seen Dodge's blood on the knife was a memory she'd never forget.

She hated herself for being the catalyst of horror in his life. Well, that was something she intended to fix. And very soon.

In a quiet moment, she'd slipped upstairs to their room and accompanied by Kaylee who wouldn't leave her side, packed their bags and stowed them in the rental car. Kaylee had been quiet and tearful about leaving. Tessa believed she was too shaken by her recent experience to fully understand they wouldn't be coming back to Bindarra Creek.

"I thought you'd left town," Dodge was saying to Sara when Tessa walked back into the drawing-room, her knees shaking under her jeans and with her daughter at her side. He winged a thoughtful glance their way from where he sprawled on the lounge and examined them. No smile. His face deadpan, he turned back to his ex-partner.

The knife in her heart twisted a little more.

The room seemed full of people with a few faces she didn't recognise and who eyed her with avid curiosity. Tessa hugged Kaylee closer and remained near the door.

Probing the bandage above her eye from where her head had met the windscreen, Sara muttered, "I intended to but I needed petrol. I crossed the river on that bridge to the north of town and was filling up when this car drove into the yard. You know what it's like Dodge. Once a cop, always a cop. Dunno what it was that sent my cop instinct on red-alert but it happened the moment this guy stepped out of his car."

"Well, I'm bloody glad you were here, Sara. We can't..." His jaw worked furiously for a minute. "We'll never be able to repay you for what you did."

"Like I said, once a cop..." She shrugged then winced. "I ache all over."

"Go on, Sara. I want to hear what happened," urged Edwina, her plastered leg propped up on a stool. She took a big gulp of her mug of tea heavily laced with scotch from the smell of it.

"You didn't see this in your tea leaves, Gran?"

Edwina grinned and winked at Dodge. "It's an unwritten rule amongst us psychics, never mention the bad stuff."

Mrs Brown entered the room from the kitchen, bearing a platter of finger-food and huffed out an irritated breath at Edwina's statement. After placing the platter on the coffee table, she sat down next to her sister.

"I could tell he meant trouble, so I followed him after he'd filled up. I didn't like the way he cruised around the town as if searching for something or someplace in particular. Then when he pulled into an abandoned house, I knew he was up to no good. I decided to follow suit. Easy enough to do, considering the number of empty houses in this place." Sara crunched on a carrot stick. "I found one where I could get my car into the back yard and out of view of the street and broke inside. So glad I brought my sleeping bag with me. Shit, this place is cold. All I did was follow him every time he moved."

Lou blew her nose on a man-sized handkerchief then stuffed it into a pocket. Her hand rested on her bulging stomach as she said, "You did good, Pyeon. I'll make sure the nobs up the chain hear about it. I know a few people. I'm certain they'll take into account your heroic actions last night when your trial comes up."

Dodge said gruffly, "In fact, I'll make damn well certain they do. I've contacted my uncle.

He's a barrister and he's going to represent you and look into your case. You're not going to be alone in this, I'll back you up. We'll find out who took that missing money too. I was going to do it anyway, even before all this happened."

"Thanks." Sara scrubbed at the single tear the dripped down her left cheek then pushed to her feet. "This time, I really am going back to Sydney. I'm driving Tessa's rental back seeing how my old Commodore is totaled."

She held out her hand to Dodge who stood as well and gripped it hard.

"You sure you're okay to drive?"

"Dodge, I can't wait to see this town in my rear vision mirror."

They grinned at each other.

"Don't be a stranger, Sara," said Edwina, raising her mug high in a salute.

Sara turned to Tessa who'd remained standing all this time and who had her arms wrapped tight around Kaylee where she leaned against her legs. "You ready?"

Wordlessly, Tessa nodded. Now that it had come to this moment, she couldn't believe how hard it was to say goodbye. Her gaze travelled the room, imprinting in her memory each dear face, even Edwina and her henchwoman, Mrs Brown. The kind Mrs Miller stared back at her, worry etched deep in her face and with her rector husband by her side sipping his tea.

Maki sitting beside Miss Collins and holding her hand, looked so sad she had to choke down a sob. He nodded. He understood. He'd always understood.

"Bloody hell! Wait a moment." Dodge stared at Tessa. "What's going on?"

"I'm leaving. We discussed this, remember?" she croaked. Bending her head, she murmured to her daughter, "Come on, sweetheart, its time."

"I don't want to go," sobbed Kaylee.

The desolation in her daughter's voice twisted the screws inside Tessa until she thought she'd fall apart from the agony. "I know but we have to. We don't belong here."

"Yes, you do. You belong with me. Both of you," Dodge ground out. His hands had fisted at his sides.

She couldn't bear to look at him but she had to make him understand. He deserved a better woman than she was and now that he knew the truth, he'd forget her. He'd move on and one day, he wouldn't even remember her name.

But she couldn't leave without telling these lovely people the sordid part she had played.

So out it came.

What had happened all those years ago, her mother and how Tessa had run away to live on the streets, her panic when she learned that low-life had found her again, her reluctant plan to fund a new life for her daughter and herself with the grant money, all the dirty, sneaky lies she'd told.

She kept her gaze on the floor, waiting. But no one said anything.

Then in the profound silence that filled the room, Tessa and Kaylee walked out the door.

In the hall, she heard Mrs Brown declare, "You remember my wedding dress, Edwina?"

"Of course I do. I'm not senile."

"I knew I kept it for a reason."

Lips shaking, Tessa smiled as she choked back her tears. These people were crazy. Wonderful, but crazy.

The last person she heard as she stepped onto the verandah was Edwina saying loudly, "Thank the Lord, those bloody shadows are gone. I can finally see the rainbow. I'm glad I don't have to draw you a picture this time, boy. Maki, stop canoodling Beatrix and get another bottle of champagne."

***

Each step she took further away from Dodge, resounded inside her body like drum beats. They reached Tessa's rental car parked in the drive. Hugging her waist and hopping from foot to foot was Sara, her breath tiny puffs of warm cloud in the frosty air. Her gaze travelled beyond Tessa and she raised her eyebrows.

"Wait! Tessa wait."

Dodge. Why couldn't he let her leave already?

Her hand curled into a fist. She shut her eyes. *Why was he making this so hard?* Unless, he'd come out to tell her exactly what he thought of her. Or he'd changed his mind and intended to get the town to press charges.

"Mummy?" asked Kaylee.

Bracing herself, she opened her eyes.

He was standing right there, in her personal space, planting his hands either side of her on the car and damn well making sure she didn't bolt until he'd had his say. There was a determined glint in his eyes that sent her body quivering with love and longing. Dare she hope?

Her chin came up.

And his mouth came down.

Hard.

Demanding.

Insistent.

And helplessly, her arms slid around his neck. She pressed herself close and kissed him back as if her life depended on it.

His lips left hers, slowly.

"As Gran says, sometimes people do the wrong thing, for the right reason. I understand now that not everything is clear cut and despite our best intentions, all of us can make bad decisions." He smiled and wiped tears from her face with his thumbs. "We can make this work. Stay with me, Tessa. Please. I want us to start again."

"Last night you wanted nothing to do with me."

"Never." He shook his head. "I needed time to think it all through. That's the way I am. I've always known in my heart you're the girl for me. But no more secrets and no more straying from the straight and narrow."

His sparkling eyes offered a glorious future if she dared reach out and take it. No recriminations. No judgement. Well, she'd never been one to turn down a promising opportunity when she saw it.

"Done. You've shown me how to share my life and to trust. You've given me so much, Dodge."

"Not as much as you've given me." He shook his head. "I almost lost you, Tessa. I'm not going to risk that happening again."

Smiling through her tears, Tessa cupped his face in her hands and said, "You have to admit, it was the best idea of my life. It brought me to you."

Dodge picked her up and carrying her away from the car, whirled her around and around to the sound of her daughter's laughter. "Darlin'," Dodge drawled. "Trust me. You haven't seen anything yet."

~The End~

Thank you so much for taking the time to read my story *Bindarra Creek Makeover* which is part of the **Bindarra Creek Romance series**.

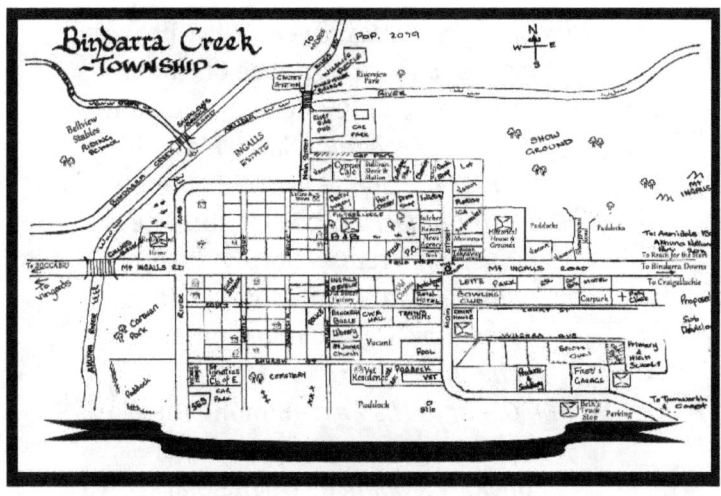

~

A little about the Bindarra Creek Romance series:
13 romances. 13 authors. 13 months.

Welcome to Bindarra Creek, a struggling country town where people work hard and love deeply. Set in the picturesque tablelands of New England, Australia, Bindarra Creek is a fictional, drought stricken community full of intrigue, adventure, drama and romance.
Life and love in a small country town has never been more challenging.

~

Books in the Bindarra Creek Romance series:

Bindarra Creek Makeover - S. E. Gilchrist
Shadows of the Heart - Lee Christine
Second Chance Love - Susanne Bellamy
The CEO Mechanic - Sandie James
Reach for the Stars - Kerrie Paterson
Home to Bindarra Creek - Juanita Kees
Stolen Sanctuary - Stacey Nash
Tempting Fate - Erin Moira O'Hara
One More Day - Linda Charles
The Vine - Lauren K. McKellar
The Ghost of His Past - Simone Angela
Joanie's Dilemma - Marianne Theresa
Buckley's Chance - Noelle Clark

For more info on the other stories in this series, please visit:
www.bindarracreekromance.com

*

BIO

S.E. Gilchrist can't remember a time when she didn't have a book in her hand. Now she dreams up stories where her favourite words are...'what if' and 'where'? SE lives in the Hunter Valley, Australia with her family and is the author of over fifteen books. Her stories are set in the exciting worlds of science fiction, ancient worlds, apocalyptic settings and contemporary small towns. SE takes a keen interest in the environment and animal welfare and loves bushwalking and Zumba.
SE is published by Escape Publishing and Momentum Books and is an indie author.

*

From the author:
Reviews can help readers find books and increase a writer's visibility. I am grateful for all honest reviews. Thank you to any who have the time to let others know what you've read and what you thought of the book.

If you'd like to know more about me, my books or to connect online, please visit my website:
www.segilchrist.com

Follow me on facebook:
https://www.facebook.com/segilchrist.19

My twitter handle is: @segilchrist1

*